Waking Up to *Love*

EVAN PURCELL

CRIMSON ROMANCE

F+W Media, Inc.

Published by
Crimson Romance
an imprint of F+W Media, Inc.
10151 Carver Road, Suite 200
Blue Ash, OH 45242. U.S.A.
www.crimsonromance.com

ISBN 10: 1-4405-8240-8
ISBN 13: 978-1-4405-8240-0
eISBN 10: 1-4405-8239-4
eISBN 13: 978-1-4405-8239-4

Cover art © 123RF/ Graham Oliver

Chapter One

It had been eleven minutes, 900 heartbeats, and four sips of bottled water since Ramona Scapizi had crawled into bed, and sleep was more elusive than ever. This was just going to be one of those nights.

She thought about switching on the lamp and reading another chapter of *Anna Karenina*, but she knew that wasn't going to work. Like most English majors, reading didn't make her the least bit sleepy. If anything, reading another ten pages of that book would only make her more depressed.

Or angry.

Or glad she wasn't Russian.

Tree branches pounded against her window. Thunder rumbled the glass. Storms were always so much more unnerving when she was alone. It had been storming a lot lately. She had been alone a lot lately, too.

This was early May in Arizona. They weren't supposed to have storms like this, at least not now. In a way, it was almost like the weather matched her mood.

Ramona looked over at her end table, and in the flashes of lightning, she could see a single family photo looking back at her. The plain wooden frame needed a dusting. It was always there, just inches away from her head, but lately Ramona was finding it harder and harder to look at.

The picture was from about a year ago. It showed Ramona in a light blue shirt and white top. She was beaming ear to ear. There were no bags under her eyes, no frizz in her hair. And standing right next to her—in red, always in red—was her twin sister Vanessa. Nessa and Mona, the Scapizi daughters. Nessa was Ramona's identical twin, but everyone saw her as the prettier one.

Maybe it was her makeup, or her hairstyle, or her expensive clothes. Maybe it was just the way she carried herself: with confidence, with passion.

Ramona, on the other hand, was 100 percent unglamorous. She had the same wavy hair, the same dusting of freckles, the same blue eyes. She was beautiful-ish, she thought, but she didn't have the poise and confidence of her sister.

Of course, Nessa had recently run away from her husband just weeks after their wedding, so it wasn't like her life was perfect, either.

Without realizing what she was doing, Ramona turned the picture around so it was facing the wall. She couldn't look at Nessa's smiling face, not after everything Nessa put her through.

The phone rang, cutting through the silence of her apartment. It seemed so much louder now, without any of the normal daytime noises to fight it for ear space—just the patter of rain. At first, she wanted to ignore it. No one should call this late. Then she realized that the phone call could be important. It could be Nessa, finally telling everybody where she was. Or at least it could be Nessa asking for money.

The phone kept ringing. It might have been her imagination, but Ramona could have sworn it was getting louder. Against that quivery feeling in the pit of her stomach, she picked up the phone.

"Hello?" She tried to make her voice sound sleepy and disgruntled. Instead, she sounded like a woozy Muppet.

"Ramona," a male voice said. It sounded deep—and very familiar. Her brain flipped through an address book of potential late-night callers, but she couldn't quite place the voice.

When she didn't answer, the voice quickly added, "Mo?"

Only one man had the nerve to call her that childhood nickname.

"Scott," she said. It sounded like an accusation. "Scott McInney."

When he chuckled, she knew her hunch was correct. Only Scott McInney laughed like that. Only Scott McInney had a chuckle that made anyone else in the room feel like the butt of some unsaid joke. She hadn't heard that laugh in three months, not since the wedding.

Back in first grade, when Scott stole her stuffed dinosaur, she'd thought his chuckle was mean and obnoxious. In fifth grade, when he gave her a heart-shaped box of chocolates, she'd thought his chuckle was nervous and impossibly cute. In high school, when he wrecked her dad's old Chevy, she'd thought his chuckle was doofy and immature. Now, at the ripe old age of twenty-seven, she didn't know what she thought about his chuckle, except to know that it was certainly not a sound she wanted to hear right before what would hopefully be a nice, restful sleep.

"I see you recognize my voice," Scott said. He chuckled again.

"Caller ID," she lied. "Don't flatter yourself."

"I'm actually not on my phone," he said. "This is the hospital's."

"Oh God," she said. "Is something wrong?"

Was he hurt now, too? His family had been through so much during the last few months. No matter how she felt about Scott, she always had a soft spot for the McInney clan; they didn't deserve to face another accident or illness.

"Oh no, no," he said. "Just the opposite. It's Mom!"

Debra McInney had been in a coma for the last two and a half months. It was a car accident on the way home from Harvey's Diner. She'd had a pancake craving, and she hadn't wanted to let her family know that she was cheating on her diet. The temporary lapse in will power had cost her three broken ribs, a sprained wrist, and eighty-four days of deep sleep.

"Scott," Ramona said. "Is your Mom—?"

"Yes!" he said. "She's awake!"

She's awake. Ramona had spent months waiting to hear those words. Now that she had, her heart swelled and her tear ducts puckered. Suddenly, her entire history with the McInney family flashed before her eyes. It was like a near-death experience, without the pesky dying part.

She saw all the mornings when she and her sister sneaked into their backyard to play pranks on Scott and his big brother, Rob. One summer alone, they'd managed to go through six rubber spiders, three packets of Halloween blood, and one surprisingly realistic pile of fake vomit.

She saw the Sunday dinners when Mrs. McInney invited Nessa and her over for some of the best home-cooked meals she'd ever had. Eating plateful after plateful of McInney mashed potatoes was so much better than dinners at home, back when her parents were constantly fighting and threatening divorce.

She saw the long nights she spent up in Scott's treehouse. Back then, it was just her and Scott, talking about life and love, talking about the future. There may have been a few rubber spiders, too.

She saw the night her dad left them. Rather than cry alone in her room, she went over to the McInney house and they cheered her up with charades. It was four in the morning.

She saw the afternoon Scott finally swallowed his pride, and asked out—Ramona's twin sister. Worse, she saw the moment exactly one month later, when he proposed.

She saw Nessa's and Scott's wedding by the beach. It was so perfect, so sickeningly perfect. No one expected Nessa to run off three weeks later.

All of the little flashes added up to an entire life of love, and anger, and frustration. No matter what happened between them, Ramona would always treasure her childhood memories with the McInneys. Sure, they hurt to think about, but life was meant to hurt sometimes, right? She didn't know exactly how she felt about Scott—never had—but she sure knew he was forever a part of her life, even if she hadn't had an argument-free conversation with him in forever.

"Ramona? Hello?" Scott's words finally brought her back into reality.

"I'm sorry," she said. "I'm just … this is such wonderful news."

"So?" he asked. "Can you come to the hospital?"

There were so many things Ramona didn't know. She didn't know why Scott had chosen her sister. She didn't know why her sister had decided to leave him. She didn't even know where her sister was anymore.

But despite all of her confusion about the past, there was one thing Ramona Scapizi knew for sure: She was definitely not going to get any sleep tonight.

Chapter Two

Scott couldn't stop staring at the beeping heart monitor. It didn't look like it was supposed to. It didn't look like the heart monitors that you see in the movies. The line was much too flat, and its spikes were irregular at best. Debra stirred in her bed, but her eyes didn't quite focus on anything.

After a few minutes, the hospital room had faded from his sight, and the only thing he could see or hear was that stupid beeping line. To him, it felt like a life, like his mother's life. If only he could push a few buttons and make it strong and steady again.

"What do you remember about the accident?"

Those words yanked Scott out of his haze. He looked around the room, at the white walls, at the posters of happy, healthy patients, at his brother Rob sitting on the other side of the hospital bed.

"Do you remember anything at all?" Rob asked again.

Their mother struggled to think. She rolled her head to look at Rob. "Pancakes," she muttered.

Yes! She remembered the pancakes.

"Good," Rob said. "That's good. Now, do you remember what happened after you left the restaurant?"

Debra McInney didn't answer. Scott couldn't tell if she was thinking, or if she didn't understand the question. Finally, she said, "I already told the doctor everything."

"We know," Rob said. "We just want to hear it, too. What happened after the restaurant?"

"I woke up," she said. "Here."

"Good," Rob said. "That's good. That's very good."

Scott wanted to scream. That wasn't good. That wasn't good at all. His mother was in a hospital bed, her heart monitor was barely moving, and she had no idea that she'd lost two and a half months of her life.

As a park ranger for the Bureau of Land Management, Scott McInney spent his more hectic days searching for lost campers or making sure drug smugglers didn't pass through his turf on their way up from the Mexican border. It was a tough job, but he was always in control. Even with last year's massive brush fire, he'd been the first man on the scene, giving orders and making decisions. Here, in this tiny hospital room, he couldn't make any decisions of his own. He couldn't just give an order and make his mother better again. He was helpless, as helpless as Debra McInney, and it scared him.

As if to respond to Scott's worries, Debra's voice became clearer and more lucid. She said, "I've been asleep a long time, haven't I?"

"A very long time," Scott said. She'd slept through her birthday. She'd slept through Scott's separation and Rob's company laying off half its employees. She'd slept through some bad months.

"Scott," Debra said. "Are you okay? You look pale."

Scott laughed out loud. Only his mother would wake up from a coma and instantly start worrying about *his* health. "Mom. I'm fine."

"I'm sure you are," she said. "I hope you didn't worry about me too much."

"No," Scott said. "I think we worried just the right amount." He didn't mention that "just the right amount" meant every single night for the last few months.

"We're good," Rob added. Scott saw the fake smile plastered on his brother's face; he worried that he looked the same way. He didn't want his mom to think they were keeping things from her.

"So where are your families?" Debra asked.

Rob and Scott exchanged glances. Scott knew he was going to tell her about Nessa leaving him sooner or later, but he was definitely hoping for the later option. He certainly didn't want to drop that bomb on her just minutes after she woke up.

"Um," Scott said. "The thing is …"

Before he could finish, Rob's seven-year-old son, Jeffrey, ran into the hospital room. He had a half-melted ice cream bar in his hand. "Grandma! Grandma!" he shouted. "Since you're awake, I got you an ice cream bar to make you feel better." The dessert had several bite marks in it already. "I had to taste it to make sure it was okay," he added.

Debra tried to sit up. "Honey," she said. "I don't think I'm supposed to eat that. You finish it, okay?"

Jeffrey took another bite. "Thank you," he mumbled through his full mouth.

"As you can see," Rob said, "Jeffrey here has grown a whole inch since you last saw him."

"I could tell!" Debra said. "He's almost a grown-up."

In truth, Jeffrey was much smaller than other boys his age. Any growth for him would only serve to help him catch up to his peers. Still, he looked so proud of himself when his grandma said "grown-up." He beamed through the ice cream stains on his face.

Scott thought that he was finally free of any Nessa questions, but his mother pressed the issue again. "And how is your lovely wife these days?" Debra asked.

Scott looked away. His marriage to Nessa Scapizi was the biggest mistake of his life. Not only did it flame out spectacularly, but he didn't even know where she was. She'd just packed her bags and left. Besides, he'd also lost his best friend. Since the proposal, Nessa's sister Ramona had been cold, distant. She probably thought it was his fault that Nessa ran away. Since the separation, Scott had only talked with Ramona a handful of times, including tonight's phone call. She seemed colder to him now, harder to talk to. He missed that connection. He missed being able to tell her anything.

Somehow, losing Ramona as a friend hurt even more than losing Nessa as a lover. He had no idea where exactly he'd taken the wrong path, but he was certainly far, far away from where his life was supposed to be.

"Nessa is fine, Mom," Scott lied.

Both Rob and Jeffrey looked at him like he'd grown a third nostril in the middle of his forehead. He gave them each a warning look.

"That's good," Debra said. Her voice was weaker again. "All I really care about is that my boys are happy."

Scott put on a big fake smile. If that was all she cared about, then she was in for a world of disappointment.

. . .

Ramona ran through the hospital lobby, accidentally clipping a nurse with her elbow. She plowed into the stairwell and charged up three flights of stairs.

She knew that Debra McInney's room was somewhere on the fourth floor. She'd visited her at least once a week since the accident, but for some reason, she couldn't remember which room she was looking for. Her mind was blank.

That didn't stop her from rushing, though. It didn't stop her from running around the corner, past the information desk, and straight into an unsuspecting doctor.

"Hello?" he said as his clipboard clattered to the ground.

The man's name tag said "Dr. Ben Nguyen." Ramona stared at his chest, re-reading his name tag several times. She had no idea what else to do.

"Can I help you?" he asked.

"Coma," she said. "McInney. Hospital." She couldn't make out full sentences. In fact, she could barely make out full words. When she said "hospital," it sounded like "popsicle."

The doctor narrowed his eyes, clearly trying to decipher what she meant.

A flush of embarrassment crept across Ramona's face. *Let's try this again,* she thought to herself. She waited for her breathing to catch up with her, she steadied herself, and she said, "I'm here to see Debra McInney. She just woke up from a coma."

Dr. Nguyen's eyes lit up. Ramona could tell that he was more than happy to give her the good news. "She's right in there," he said, pointing toward room 418.

Ramona paused for a moment to appreciate Dr. Nguyen's genuinely happy smile. Why couldn't she be best friends with someone like that? Maybe if she had grown up next door to him instead of someone like Scott, a nature-loving adventurer who never gave her the time of day, she'd be a happier person.

She realized that she was staring at Dr. Nguyen. He was busy picking up his fallen clipboard and reading the chart.

Farber City Memorial Hospital was the only hospital to serve their small river town, so naturally it was filled with people. The waiting rooms were packed with patients from all walks of life: businessmen, construction workers, housewives, college students. Ramona passed a waiting room that was one Indian short of a Village People concert.

She came to a door with the numbers 4-1-8 etched on a small gold plaque. This was it. Debra McInney was in here. Did Ramona really want to do this? Sure, she loved Debra like a mother, but if she pushed the door open, she'd have to see Scott, too. Was it really worth all the awkwardness?

An image flashed through her mind: She was six, and Debra McInney was putting a Flintstones bandage on her cut knee. She loved Debra so much.

Ramona pushed open the door. At first, all she saw was the small, frail woman attached to so many tubes and machines. No matter how many times she'd visited Debra, she never got used to seeing Debra look so weak. Then Ramona saw the two McInney brothers waiting by her side. Rob looked the same as always: blond, skinny, a little doofy. He had the telltale forehead crinkles of someone who had spent the last few months worrying about his sick mother, and his struggling business, and his seven-year-old son. Clearly Rob was tired all the way down to his bones, but trying not to show it.

Jeffrey sat on his father's lap. He was asleep, but judging from the ice cream smudges on his cheeks, he must've just fallen asleep. Lucky kid.

And of course, there was Scott. Normally, his face was the first thing Ramona noticed when she entered a room. His was the face she had grown up with. She could always read those expressive gray eyes, that half-smirking grin. Scott McInney was a park ranger for BLM and he looked the part, all six feet, two inches of him. His wide frame was edged with muscles, but he didn't have the body of someone who spent hours at the gym; his imposing figure came courtesy of a job that had him laying pipe, digging fences, and carrying heavy loads of dirt and rock. He looked strong, and he looked completely comfortable in his own skin.

Scott waved at Ramona, and she forgot how a simple wave from Scott McInney could make her heart shimmy in her chest.

Debra struggled to move her head to the side. Her eyes were still half shut and her mouth was scrunched up in a grimace. The instant she saw Ramona, though, her eyes lit up and the corners of her mouth curled upward. "Why, hello," she said.

Ramona half waved awkwardly. "Hello," she said. "You look great." She didn't entirely mean that. Debra's color was still off and she'd lost a lot of weight during the coma. However, she was moving, and she was smiling.

"Doesn't she?" Scott said. He placed his hand on his mother's.

"So how are you feeling?" Ramona asked.

Scott answered for her. "Her vitals are up," he said, "and the doctor is coming back to—"

"Scott!" Debra snapped. She gave him one of her patented McInney warning glances, the kind that basically said, "Don't test me!!" with two exclamation marks.

"Mom?" Scott asked.

"I can speak for myself, son," she said. Her expression instantly softened. It reminded Ramona of the Debra she'd known before the accident, the Debra she'd known all her life. This was a woman who was never afraid to take charge. She was quick to scold, but she never did it out of anger.

"It's nice to see that you haven't changed, Mrs. McInney," Ramona said.

"Same to you," she said. "Now come closer so I can get a better look at my favorite daughter-in-law."

Uh-oh.

Ramona gulped. She realized with a sudden rush of horror that Debra thought she was her twin sister Nessa.

Double uh-oh.

Ramona realized with a second gulp that Debra thought her son was still married. She exchanged glances with Scott, hoping he could see the look of icy fear etched across her face. She was close to Debra McInney, but she didn't feel right delivering such personal news to her.

Should she correct her? Should she at least say that she was Ramona and not Nessa?

Ramona knew that Scott could sense her panic, but he wasn't responding. In fact, he diverted his eyes and started staring at a poster on the wall. It showed a healthy blond family having a picnic. Since he wasn't helping her out, she only had one choice. She had to tell Debra the truth. "Actually, Mrs. McInney," she said. "I—"

"Please call me Debra," she corrected. "We're family, remember?"

Gulp.

All their lives, Debra McInney had looked out for Ramona and her sister. She loved them like daughters. She loved them each individually, even if she could never quite tell them apart.

"Yes," she said. "Well, that's the thing ..."

Before she could finish her sentence, Dr. Nguyen walked into the room. He was smiling again. He looked like the kind of doctor from a medication commercial, blandly handsome and pleasant.

"Oh good," he said. "Everybody's here."

Everybody except my MIA sister, Ramona thought.

"Okay," the doctor continued. "Can all the family members meet with me outside for a sec?" In response to Debra's panicked expression, he quickly added, "Nothing serious."

No one moved.

"Family members? Please?" Dr. Nguyen said.

Scott and Rob both walked out into the hallway with the doctor. Rob carefully set his son on the empty chair, making sure not to wake him. Ramona stayed behind, staring once again at Debra. In the new silence, Debra's heart monitor sounded extremely loud.

"Well?" Debra asked.

"Yes?"

"Aren't you going to join them?" she asked. "You are part of the family now, aren't you?"

It was now two forty-five on a Tuesday morning. She was in no condition to make any major decisions right now. If she thought about it logically, she could have easily said, "Actually, I'm Ramona, not Nessa. I'll just wait here with you." It was that simple. Of course, Ramona had just run out of her supply of logic for the week. Besides, it was two forty-five a.m. No one is logical at two forty-five a.m.

So Ramona nodded, said, "I'll be right back," and walked out into the hallway.

"… and there's not much more we can do in the hospital," Dr. Nguyen was telling the brothers. His smile was still there, but it was slowly fading.

"So she's going to be fine?" Scott asked.

Dr. Nguyen nodded. "There's no reason to think otherwise. However, it will be a long road to recovery, and her heart is extremely weak."

Ramona thought back to the beeping heart monitor. It sounded so faint, so quiet.

"But I thought you put her on medications to help fix that," Rob said.

"We did," the doctor answered. "But it'll take some time for her heart to go back to full strength. She's out of the woods for now, but any big surprises, especially in these first weeks, could be … well, they could be deadly."

Ramona felt herself recoil. Deadly? Any surprises?

"You mean like a divorced son?" Scott asked blankly.

Dr. Nguyen's smile had completely faded. In its place was a look both calm and professional. "Would she be shocked by the news?" he asked.

Rob and Scott nodded.

"Our mom doesn't believe in divorce," Rob said. "Besides, the circumstances were a little messy."

"Yeah," Scott added. "I married the girl next door and she ran away three weeks later. No one knows where she is." He didn't mention the fact that her identical twin sister was standing two feet away from them.

"Yes," Dr. Nguyen said. "That's definitely a conversation that you'll want to avoid."

Rob and Scott nodded again. Ramona waited for them to ask some follow-up questions, but neither said anything.

"So what should we do?" Ramona blurted out. After the words came out of her mouth, she realized how presumptuous it was to use the word "we." There was no "we." There never was a "we."

"Well," the doctor said, "she'll be back here in two weeks for more tests. If all her vitals are fine, you can tell her everything then."

"Two weeks?" Rob said. "That's all?"

"Seems easy enough," Scott said.

Rob excused himself to go back into the room and check on Debra.

Dr. Nguyen looked at Scott and Ramona, waiting for any more questions. When neither of them said anything, he told them, "I'll print out a list of instructions for her care. It won't be too difficult, mainly keeping close watch at all times and making sure she doesn't suffer any unexpected shocks. But I would like to say that she seems to be in the right hands. You all seem to genuinely care for her."

He walked away.

Ramona started to walk back into room 418, but Scott stopped her. "Wait," he said.

Ramona twisted out of his grip. His fingers were scratchy and calloused, as they had always been. Even when they were children, long before he started working with his hands, she'd thought his fingers were rough. That part about him hadn't changed. In so many little ways, he was the same Scott he always was.

She felt her pulse quicken at his touch. This was the child who'd played games with her, the boy who'd watched out for her, and the man who'd left her behind, all in the same frustrating package. She didn't want her heart to flutter. She didn't want the corners of her mouth to instinctively curl into a smile. Most of all, she didn't want his touch to feel so comfortable, so warm, so right.

"I need to ask you something," he said. "Something very important."

He leaned forward until they were the same height. His expression was dead serious, and whatever he was going to ask her, he meant it. For an extremely long second, Ramona thought he was leaning in to kiss her.

He didn't. Instead, he looked her straight in the eyes and asked, "Can you pretend to be your sister? At least for a few days?"

Ramona thought about it for ten seconds. Her heart beat. She blinked. Finally, after ten seconds of waiting and thinking, Ramona Scapizi had her answer: "Hell, no."

Chapter Three

Ramona needed to catch her breath. She needed some air. Unfortunately, she was in the middle of the fourth floor of Farber City Memorial Hospital. It wasn't like there was a park within walking distance. Mostly, though, she wanted to get away from Scott McInney and his begging eyes. She would not fake-marry him. She would not pretend to be her twin.

Before he could say anything else, she ran down the hall and straight into the nearest waiting room. Here, surrounded by so many strangers, Scott wouldn't dare make a spectacle of himself.

The waiting room smelled like used Band-Aids and window cleaner. Ramona was suddenly aware of her surroundings, and those surroundings were anything but pleasant. An old lady sat in a corner, nursing what looked like a broken arm. A Hispanic couple sat with their five-year-old son, rubbing his back as he coughed up a lung and a half. A skinny guy had a gash in his shoulder, a teen girl was half asleep against the wall, and a housewife had her husband holding an ice pack against her eye.

Scott rushed into the waiting room after her. He had that same pleading look on his face.

"Ramona," he said, holding up an invisible ring, "will you please do me the honor of being my pretend wife?"

Ramona couldn't think straight. This was not the place for thinking. This was not the place for relaxing. This certainly wasn't the place for Scott to get down on one knee and fake-propose to her.

Apparently "hell no" wasn't a strong enough answer. She probably should've added a few more swear words, or a slap.

"Scott, please," she whispered to him.

He remained on his knee. "Ramona Scapizi," he said, louder than ever, "please say yes."

Everyone in the waiting room turned their attention to her. The woman with the black eye even pulled away her ice pack so she could get a better look. The people in this waiting room were struggling with their own problems and sicknesses; watching a marriage proposal would help them forget about all that, if only for a few minutes.

Ramona felt her cheeks flush with warmth. She wanted to say no, she *needed* to say no for her own sanity. But all those eyes were staring at her, and Scott had a surprisingly genuine expression on his face.

"Say yes!" the Hispanic kid shouted. He stopped coughing.

The old lady with the broken arm was crying now. It was presumably because of her shattered ulna, but watching this grand gesture probably didn't help.

"I'm sorry, guys," Ramona said to the crowd. "This isn't what it looks like. You did hear him say 'pretend,' right?"

"Say yes," the boy shouted again, and pretty soon he was joined by his parents. "Say yes! Say yes!"

Then the wife with the ice pack started shouting. Then her husband. "Say yes! Say yes! Say yes!" Before Ramona knew it, everyone in the waiting room, and a few of the nurses behind the counter, were all urging her to accept his proposal. It seemed like the only person opposed to this idea was Ramona herself.

She tried to argue with them. She shouted, "But he married my sister!" No one heard her, though. They just chanted louder.

"Say yes! Say yes! Say yes! Say yes!"

After two whole minutes of complete strangers chanting and shouting and laughing and coughing at her, Ramona finally threw her hands in the air. "Fine," she mumbled. "I'll fake-marry you."

Scott turned to the crowd. "She said yes!" he shouted.

The waiting room burst into applause.

Scott got to his feet and slipped his invisible wedding ring onto her finger.

She squinted and pretended to study the ring. She made a face, as if its diamond was much too small for her taste. She was about to say something snarky, but Scott grabbed her by the waist and dipped her backwards. He was going to kiss her.

When his face got dangerously close to hers, she muttered, "You kiss me, you die."

He kissed her on the cheek. She slugged him in the arm. Hard.

• • •

Scott led his "wife" back into Room 418, or at least that was what he told himself. In actuality, she was a good three steps ahead of him, and she only paused so that he could open the door for her. Oh, Ramona; she hadn't changed since first grade. She was still as headstrong as ever. No imaginary jewelry, no matter how many imaginary karats it had, could change that.

"After you," he said, making a big show out of his chivalry.

Jeffrey was sitting on his dad's lap again, suddenly awake, and Debra was sitting up straight, or at least as straight as she could. Her breathing was still raggedy.

"I see everyone's come back from their secret meeting," Debra said as soon as Scott closed the door behind him. "I hope everyone's fine."

Scott couldn't help but smile to himself. It had only been a couple of hours since she woke up, but his mom was already getting her fire back.

"We spoke with the doctor," Rob explained, "and he said you're going to be just fine."

"'Course he did," Debra said. "That's the kind of news that a doctor would deliver in private."

"Mom," Rob said.

"Oh, pooh," Debra answered. That was one of her stock expressions. She had been saying that since Scott was old enough to spill his soda or forget to use a coaster. "It doesn't matter what the doctor told you, because I feel great. Fantastic. Stupendous. In fact, I feel so good that I think we should have a party for me."

"What?" Scott asked.

"A welcome back party," she explained. "Or more of a 'good morning' party. Don't you think that's appropriate?"

The room fell silent.

"After all," she said, "I *did* miss my birthday, didn't I?"

"Yeah," Scott said.

"So what do you say? A good morning party?"

Scott couldn't help but notice that she was looking directly at Ramona when she asked that. He didn't know why. Was his mother already seeing through the charade? He couldn't bear to have his mother find out he'd lied to her less than an hour after she woke up.

"I think that's very appropriate," Rob chimed in from his corner of the room.

Debra pretended not to hear him. She had her eyes firmly set on Ramona, on her fake daughter-in-law. "Nessa?" she asked again.

"Sure," Ramona muttered. "I think that's … a good idea."

Scott knew that tone. He knew Ramona wasn't being completely truthful. Then again, he was the one who'd asked her to lie in the first place.

"Great," Debra exclaimed. "Nessa and I will start planning the party tomorrow, as soon as my boys take me home."

Scott breathed a sigh of relief. His mother didn't recognize Ramona after all. The relief was short-lived, though, because he quickly realized that his fake wife was going to be spending a lot more time at the McInney house. This was going to be more difficult than he thought.

"Um, Mom," Scott said, "I don't think—"

"I think it's a great idea!" Ramona chimed in.

Debra looked at her son. "See? Your wife agrees with me."

Chapter Four

As Ramona walked down the hospital hallway, she saw Dr. Nuygen talking with a trio of nurses. She didn't want him to see her, so she crept along the edge of the hallway until she reached the corner.

Don't see me, she prayed. *Don't see me. Don't see me.*

He didn't.

She needed to call her work and tell them that she couldn't make it tomorrow. She was going to use her cell phone, but she knew that would be a big hospital no-no. Surely the waiting room had a public phone she could use instead.

The one nurse on duty acknowledged her with a blank stare and a non-smile.

"Excuse me," Ramona said.

No answer.

Ramona had never seen someone look more disinterested. It made sense. If you were constantly surrounded by emergencies and death, it stood to reason that anything non-life-threatening would feel unimportant.

"Ma'am?" Ramona tried again.

"Is there a problem?" the nurse asked.

"Yes … no. I was wondering if I could use your phone to call my work. I want to make sure—"

"Don't you have a cell phone?" the nurse asked. She shuffled through some papers that might have been a patient file, or they might have been randomly selected sheets of nothing to keep her hands occupied.

"Well," Ramona said, "I thought I wasn't supposed to use a cell phone here. You know."

"Why?" the nurse asked.

Ramona didn't know what to say. She'd never understood the rule anyway. "Uh, it interferes with equipment … and stuff. I don't know."

"I believe you're thinking about planes," the nurse said.

She couldn't tell whether that was a joke. "Okay, then. Well, I'll use my cell phone … in the waiting room. Great."

Ramona waited for the nurse to give her approval. A nod. Anything. When she didn't, Ramona left.

Thankfully, most of the people who'd been in the waiting room earlier—those who'd witnessed the "proposal"—were gone now. Not so thankfully, the news had spread pretty quickly. One of the newbies shouted, "Hey! It's marriage girl!" and another one said, "Aww. That's great."

With one hand, she covered her ear. With the other, she called the office.

Because it was now about three thirty in the morning, her call went straight to voicemail. "Nancy. Hey. It's Ramona. I know you won't get this till tomorrow morning, but I'm going to have to take a personal day. I have some … family matters to deal with." She wondered if she needed to add anything else. A more thorough explanation, perhaps? "Um, I'll talk to you tomorrow, because I might be taking some time off for the next couple of days. I'll keep you informed about what my schedule will be. I just … it's family stuff."

Click.

What was she doing? Was she really going to let this stupid fake marriage affect all other aspects of her life? Yeah, she was. And she might as well go all the way with it. She owed it to Debra.

"Hey."

Ramona jumped a little.

Scott stood at the edge of the waiting room. "Calling work?" he asked.

"Yeah. I left a message for Nancy. We don't have any events booked for the next month, so I should be okay." She quickly added, "For a little while, anyway."

"Great."

He smiled and she smiled and they would've kept smiling at each other if one of the nearby patients didn't shout out, "Congratulations, guys!"

Ramona instinctively stepped back a half step.

"You know," Scott said, "you can go home if you want. You should probably rest up."

She looked deep into his eyes, making sure he meant what he said. "Okay," she decided.

But was it okay? If she was going to get involved in this, if she was going to commit to the charade, was it okay to just leave like that? "Um, I'll just say goodbye to Debra, 'kay?"

Scott nodded. She headed back down the hall, and he almost followed her, but one of the waiting room people shouted out, "Congrats, man!" And Scott, for whatever reason, went over to talk to the latest adoring fan.

When Ramona reentered Room 418, she was greeted by a cloud of laughter. Rob, Jeffrey, Debra—they were all laughing. Rob even snorted a little.

"Is everything okay?" she asked. "You guys didn't break into the medicine cabinet or anything?"

Jeffrey stood up. He was completely awake now. "Grandma was just telling us about the time Uncle Scott tried to rescue a cat that didn't need rescuing."

And just like that, Ramona joined the conversation. She was a sucker for embarrassing stories from Scott's childhood, and she knew that this one was a doozy. Scott had thought the next-door neighbor's cat was stuck in a tree. Thanks to that cat—Jinx, if she wasn't mistaken—Scott still had a forearm scar.

"He was so surprised!" Rob said, laughing again.

"That's nothing," Ramona said. "Remember the time—"

Without realizing it, she sat down on the only chair left in the room. She was still going to leave, but she could wait a few minutes.

More than a few minutes later, Scott returned with some more vending machine snacks. He looked around the room. At first, Ramona thought he was surprised that she was still there. She realized, though, that he was actually trying to figure out where he was supposed to sit. He was an adult, so he could've easily asked Jeffrey to move for him. Instead, he sat next to Ramona.

The chair was wide enough for them both, except his side pressed against hers. She had to angle herself toward him. The only way for her to be completely comfortable was if she crossed one of her legs over one of his.

Whatever.

She knew that this was the type of thing she'd have to get used to. Sharing chairs. Close contact. It was all for Debra's benefit.

"Oh hey!" Rob shouted. "You remember the time Ramona and Nessa were over and they—"

While his brother started a new story, Scott whispered to Ramona, "I hope this is okay."

"It's fine," she said.

But it was more than fine. It felt good to have him so close, side to side. She felt comfortable with him there. She felt comfortable feeling his warmth.

"…you remember that, Nessa?" Rob asked.

Ramona was getting tired again, so it took her a few seconds to realize that Rob was talking to her. "Uh, yeah. Good times."

They talked and laughed for a few minutes. Scott's arm ended up around her shoulders. Her head ended up leaning against his side. And her eyes ended up closed. She fell asleep.

The next thing she knew, early morning sunlight streamed in through the hospital windows. All night, she had slept in Scott's arms.

...

Scott's old truck bounced down the road, and Ramona could feel every pothole and bump. The streets around the hospital were reasonably well paved, or at least well paved by Arizona standards, but the old Chevy made it feel like they were on the cratered surface of the moon.

Ramona wasn't prone to getting carsick, but she felt a little greener nonetheless.

"You still like working at the library?" Scott asked.

"Uh-huh," Ramona said. She wasn't in the mood for small talk right now, mostly because she kept thinking about all the stuff she'd have to do in the next week, but also because of the general stomach queasiness.

"That was always the perfect place for you," he said, seemingly unaware of his passenger's slow transition from pink to green. "Quiet, peaceful, relaxed."

"Uh-huh."

Finally, they turned onto Highway 95, the main street through town. Thanks to the traffic, the truck slowed down to a crawl. Ramona could relax.

"I'm not saying you're quiet and peaceful," Scott explained. "But you've always loved your books. And I—"

"Let's just sort through a couple of things first," Ramona cut him off.

"Definitely not relaxed," Scott mumbled to himself, even though Ramona could clearly hear him.

"Look, Scott. I'm doing you a favor. A big one. And if I'm going to get through this alive—"

At the word "alive," Scott rammed his foot onto the brake and Ramona pitched forward. They reached a red light.

"We need to set up some rules," she continued. "I need to know exactly what you want from me."

"Okay," he said. He looked straight ahead. When they were in the midst of small talk, he couldn't keep his eyes off her, but now that things got serious, his eyes were glued to the road. "It's really simple. When Mom's awake and puttering around the house or whatever, I would like you to be there. As my wife."

"As Nessa," she corrected him.

"That's what I said."

It made her mad that he still couldn't tell the difference between those two things.

"I hope you don't expect me to cook," she said.

"Oh God, no."

"What's that supposed to mean?"

"It means I remember when you were in eighth-grade home ec. I remember the bubbling lab experiments you brought home for me and Rob to try."

She laughed. "They weren't that bad."

"Okay. Never mind. Just understand that there will be no cooking involved. You know my mom. As long as there are other humans in the house, she's constantly making sure stomachs are full. It's her thing."

For a second, Ramona thought she smelled a whiff of McInney chocolate-chip cookies. Then the phantom smell was gone.

"It's going to be hard, you know."

"What is?" he asked.

"Pretending to be my sister."

"Well, you already look the part." He finally looked at her this time. Just for a second. Maybe two. With two fingers, he casually pushed a strand of hair away from her face. It was instinctual. He probably didn't even know that he'd made contact. He certainly didn't realize that he'd caused her skin to tingle and her heart to shake.

"Thanks." She wasn't amused.

Scott laughed again.

God, that laugh made her remember so much, both good and bad. But right then, all she could think about was freshman year of high school, so many years ago. Puberty had just kicked into high gear for them both, and Ramona was finally starting to grapple with her feelings for Scott. Her complicated, more-than-friends feelings.

She remembered pulling him aside in between their classes. She remembered lockers slamming all around them. That day, she'd asked him why he never asked her out. They were practically joined at the hip back then. Why not take things further?

And his answer? He laughed and said he couldn't handle her. It was his way of making a joke out of something serious. And she never brought it up again.

"So I guess I'll have to start acting more like my sister now," she said.

"I guess you will."

"I am not going to get a manicure, if that's what you're thinking."

"That's not what I was thinking."

"Good," Ramona said. "So, um, how do I act more like my sister?"

Scott thought for a second. "Well, you know how to do the Nessa-laugh."

Ramona dipped her hair back and wheezed.

"That's the one," Scott said. "Kind of impressive, actually. But more important than that, you just need to act more … proper, I guess."

"Proper?"

"Yeah. Here's an example. Say you drop something under the refrigerator."

"Like what?" she asked.

"I don't know. A magnet."

"An important magnet?"

"Sure," he said. "A golden magnet. Whatever. So you, Nessa Scapizi, drop a magnet under the fridge. What do you do?"

"I get on my hands and knees and scoop it out," she said. "If I can't reach it, I'll use … a spatula."

Scott made a noise like a game show buzzer. "Sorry. Incorrect. You walk into the other room and recruit someone else to get it for you."

"But that's not right."

"That's Nessa," he said. "Think about all the times we played in the mud in elementary school. Did Nessa join us? No, she sat on the nearest rock so her dress wouldn't get dirty. Your sister would never join us when we swam in the river. She didn't help us make stink bombs. And she certainly wouldn't work at a job where she's restocking dusty books onto shelves. She is … proper."

More like uptight, Ramona thought, but she didn't say it out loud.

They passed through the center of town, seemingly hitting every red light. The air was still thick and moist from last night's rain. Early summer wind passed through their half-open windows. Since this was Arizona, early summer wind felt more like midsummer wind, like *dog-days-of-summer* wind, but Ramona couldn't complain.

Besides, Scott's A/C had died a hero's death a couple of summers ago, back when anything below triple digits was basically impossible.

"Hey, look where we are," Scott said. He pointed toward the old library building up ahead. Ramona had been working there for five years now, but even before that, she'd spent hours upon hours there reading through the new releases. Sometimes, Scott had joined her. Well, before they started high school. Before bookworms were officially uncool.

"That's my spot," Ramona said. She was proud of her little library and all the stuff it did for their community. Scott was definitely a local hero, with his various ranger adventures, but Ramona did her part, too.

She smiled.

A few seconds later, the library was nothing more than a shrinking reflection in the rearview mirror.

When they were kids, Ramona would always gravitate toward the romances first. Anything with a happy ending. Life was so complicated and nothing ever ended up the way she wanted, so it was a relief to read about characters who found their happy endings, who got what they deserved.

Scott, meanwhile, only read adventure stories. The bloodier, the better. If there was a bazooka on the cover, or a grappling hook, or a bomb, that was all he cared about.

That was probably why he'd grown up to be such an adventurer himself—

Which made Ramona think that perhaps this whole charade was just another adventure for him. Sure, he was doing it for the right reason—his mother—but surely he could've thought of something less complicated than a fake wife and a twin-swap. It was almost like he had cast her as the busty blond sidekick on the cover of one of his action novels, even though she was neither busty nor blond.

No, she thought. He wouldn't. He couldn't. He loved his mother too much for that. He respected Ramona too much for that.

The warm wind whipped through the truck. She pulled her hair back behind her ears.

Life wasn't like those novels. It was messier, more complicated. Besides, she couldn't get inside Scott's head. She'd have to assume that he was doing this for the right reasons. But no matter the reasons, she needed to set up the ground rules. Whatever type of book they were in—romance, adventure, or something in between—she had to make sure they were on the same page.

"And where exactly am I supposed to stay during this whole situation?" Ramona asked.

"At your apartment," he answered. "And I'll stay at the house."

"But your mom doesn't know that you moved back in after the wedding. How are you going to explain—?"

"I'll say that I'm staying at the house while she gets better. She doesn't have to know anything about the other house, the one that I lost." The "other house," as he described it, was the one that he and Nessa had picked out together. The little blue house with the white trim. Ramona knew that it meant a lot to him; it was his first real place outside of his childhood home. But after Nessa left—

It was just a rental anyway.

"She doesn't need to know," Scott repeated. A shadow crossed his face.

"So I'll stay at my place?" Ramona clarified.

"Unless you wanna share a room at McInney Manor," he offered.

She wouldn't dare. Talk about an unnecessary temptation. Sure, it would make more sense for their story, but she wouldn't put herself through that kind of heartache. It would be like flying too close to the sun.

"I think I'll pass," she said.

"Understandable."

"And, um, what about … public appearances?" she asked.

"What? Like parades?"

"No. I mean—"

"You won't have to make any speeches or attend any cocktail parties, if that's what you mean."

"That is not what I mean, Scott McInney. I'm talking about … we're not going to pretend to be married when your mom isn't around."

"Of course not."

Ramona breathed a sigh of relief, even if there were definitely other feelings mixed in there, too.

"This is just for Mom's benefit. When she's not around, you can do whatever you want to do. She's not going to get a lot of visitors, and the ones who do show up will be thoroughly prepped beforehand. You don't have to worry about keeping up appearances."

"Good to know."

They both smiled at each other, and for a second, it felt like old times, like the sort of comfortable silence that you only experience with someone you've known for decades.

Suddenly, Ramona realized that Scott's old, rusted Chevy had pulled into her apartment complex. The ride was over. That was it.

More importantly, the last few minutes had been on a twisting dirt road. Potholes and lumps and tree branches. She should've felt it; she should've been as sick and green as she was at the beginning of the ride. Instead—

She felt okay.

Better than okay. She felt good.

She popped the door open and unbuckled herself. "So you sure you're ready for this?" she asked.

Scott smiled at her. It was the same smile he had as a kid. The same dimples. "I'm as ready as you are."

• • •

Ramona re-fluffed the couch pillows. Rob re-stacked the coasters. Any second now, Scott and Debra would walk through that door.

"Why can't this be a surprise party?" Jeffrey said.

Rob knelt down so that he was eye-level with his son. "Because we don't want to scare Grandma's heart. We do a lot of stuff to make sure her heart is okay." With that last sentence, he made a quick side glance to Ramona.

"Also," she joined in, "surprise parties are horrible."

Ramona had less than fond memories of the surprise party Debra threw for Ramona and her sister twenty years ago. They both ran screaming from the house before anyone could tell them it was a party. Ramona would've called 9-1-1 if Scott hadn't chased after her and explained the situation.

Click.

Someone was at the front door.

"They're coming," Jeffrey proclaimed. "They're coming."

In unison, Rob, Jeffrey, and Ramona sat down on the big couch. They smiled and tried to look casual.

Scott walked in first, looking around to see if the coast was clear. Then he ushered Debra inside.

Ramona and Scott yelled, "Hello!"

Jeffrey said, "Surprise!" Actually, he whispered "surprise." Maybe that was his way of making sure his grandma was surprised, but not too surprised.

"A surprise party?" Debra said. "Thank you."

"It was my idea," Jeffrey said proudly.

Debra looked all around the living room, and she clearly liked what she saw. Good thing, too, because Ramona, Scott, and Rob had spent all morning sprucing things up and buying extra supplies for her big return.

Jeffrey ran over and tugged on Debra's dress. "Grandma. Can I give you a tour?"

Debra didn't exactly need a tour of her own house, but she accepted anyway. Jeffrey tugged her into the hallway. Rob chased after them, presumably so that the over-excited seven-year-old didn't wear out the hospital patient.

For the first time since their ride in his truck, Scott and Ramona were alone.

"You dusted," he said.

"Just a little," Ramona explained. "I figured it would take about a half hour for you to pick her up, so—"

"Thanks," he said. Before she could get too proud of herself, he added, "As long as you didn't use the lime green dust rags. Those are family heirlooms."

Gulp.

That was exactly what Ramona had used. They didn't seem like heirlooms. They seemed like dust rags.

"Um ..."

"Stop looking so scared," he said. "I'm kidding."

She shoved him in the shoulder. Hard.

"Sorry," he said, laughing. "I saw one sticking out of your back pocket, so I knew those were the ones you used. Not funny?"

"Not funny," she said.

He breathed deeply. "I still can't believe it."

"That I thought some old rag was a family heirloom?" she asked.

"That she's okay," he said. "After eighty-five days."

She hugged him, not like a wife hugging a husband, but like a friend comforting a friend. "It's surreal."

"Exactly," he said. "Surreal. If you just look at my life right now, it's almost like the last three months never happened."

"Well, not exactly," she said. There was a coldness in her voice, and she didn't know why.

"For the longest time," he continued, "I thought she'd never wake up."

"Really?"

"Yeah."

"I never gave up hope," Ramona said. "I always knew things would work out okay."

"I guess that's the difference between you and me," he said. "I'm not as hopeful."

That was certainly *a* difference between them, but it wasn't the only one. But what was she hoping for right now? His arms were wrapped around her shoulders, their breathing in perfect sync, and an embrace that started out as friendship was slowly morphing into something else.

Those old teenage feelings came back to her, full force. She didn't want to start crushing on him again, not when they were watching over his mom. Not when they were playing house.

But his embrace—so comfortable.

He pulled away first. "You can leave if you want to," he said.

"What?" she asked. His voice was perfectly clear, but she hoped that she'd misheard him.

He put a hand on her shoulder. "You can go home," he said. "I've already asked too much of you for the day."

Ramona's heart sank. Even though she knew he was doing her a favor, it felt like he was abandoning her. Again.

And just like that, her mind whirled back to the beginning of the year, before the wedding, before the coma, before everything. It was just her and Nessa, drinking tea and watching some trashy reality television (Nessa's choice, not hers).

Ramona asked her sister about her day, and that was when Nessa casually said, "Scott asked me out this morning. So I guess we're dating now."

Ramona couldn't catch her breath. She should've been happy for her sister and her best friend. But the only thing she could think of, as she struggled to process this new information, was: *Why did he choose* her?

She felt that Scott had abandoned her, even though she had no claim over him, even though he wasn't even in the same room. Ramona knew those feelings were irrational. Scott could date whomever he wanted. But it just felt—unfair. A month later, when they announced their last-minute marriage, that felt unfair, too.

And right now, after spending the morning sprucing up his house and pretending to be his wife, he pushed her away again.

Unfair.

When she hadn't budged, he repeated himself. "Seriously. I'm already asking way too much of you. You don't have to stay right now."

Without making any noise, Debra walked back into the living room. Ramona wouldn't have noticed her if she hadn't stopped a few feet away. "Rob and Jeffrey are chasing each other in the back yard," she explained. "And what are you two love birds doing?"

Ramona looked at Scott, waiting for him to respond. When he didn't, she said, "I have to go back to work."

And she certainly wasn't lying. There were still a few hours left in the workday. If she went straight there, she'd be able to meet with the staff and set a few things into place for the rest of her leave of absence.

Honestly, it was better this way.

And Debra certainly didn't look disappointed. She smiled that Debra-smile and said, "See you tomorrow!"

Ramona turned to leave. She had fulfilled her wifely duties for the day. Now it was time to return to the real world.

As she left, Scott said, "Love you!" But he was just playing the part.

• • •

Scott helped his mother get into bed. She said she didn't need the help, but she did.

Moonlight lit up the bedroom, making all of the sharp angles—dressers, cabinets, mirror edges—seem to glow a pale white. It was filled with stuff, comfortable stuff, but it also felt weirdly empty.

Debra McInney was finally back in her own bed. The room should've been full of life. It should've finally felt like the room had a purpose.

It didn't.

It was cold.

Empty.

And Debra seemed somehow lost in her blankets.

"If you need anything," Scott said, "I'll just be down the hall."

"I know where your old bedroom is."

"I know you know."

God, why couldn't she just go to sleep at night and wake up in the morning with all her problems gone? Why couldn't she just feel better?

Scott turned to leave.

"Wait," Debra called.

Clouds must've passed over the moon, because the room darkened. He couldn't make out his mother's face anymore. The shadows were too heavy.

"What is it, Mom?"

"You don't need to stay here."

"It's okay. I—"

"Seriously. You. Don't. Need. To. Stay. Here." She said it like a proclamation, like a royal decree.

"What if—"

"What if *nothing*. Go home to your wife. I'm sure she misses you."

"I don't know," he said.

"You don't know if she misses you?"

"No. She does. Miss me. But I think—"

"Scott Owen McInney."

For once, Scott was glad he couldn't see his mother's face. "Mom."

"Your wife loves you. Be with her."

What a laugh. His wife had actively fled from him. And his other wife—the fake one—was an innocent bystander roped into duping a sixty-four-year-old woman. Outside of this house, Scott didn't have anywhere to go.

"Mom," he said. "I don't know if you know this, but I've been having trouble sleeping. For a while now. Ever since your … well, since your accident. Even when I'm with R—Nessa, even when I'm with my wife, it's hard for me to stop worrying. About you. The only time I can get a good night's rest is when I'm here, close enough to help if something goes wrong. I hope you understand."

Moonlight once again broke through the clouds.

What was she going to say? He couldn't tell. He studied his mother, the way that the corners of her eyes crinkled, the way she half smiled. She had the same dimples as he did.

"You're a good son," she said.

And that was that.

Chapter Five

The Arizona sun shone high over the Colorado River. Sometimes, Scott McInney forgot how beautiful his home was. Other times—times like these—he knew exactly how beautiful it was. He took special care to notice the dramatic rock formations, the light blue sky, and the clusters of ducks watching him curiously. This land was a paradise, and if he just appreciated it long enough, he would stop thinking about Ramona.

Scott's muscular body was crouched like a warrior on the makeshift dock his crew had made last week. Under the dock, the river itself rushed and churned. As always, the rest of his crew was by his side: new guy Miguel, ex-surfer dude Terry, and retired Navy vet Quinn.

"Hey, bro," Terry said to no one in particular. "Hand me a pocketknife, 'kay? This branch is too long."

All four men worked tirelessly over piles of donated Christmas trees, some plastic pipe, and coils of twine. As the only BLM crew in the Farber City area, their territory included most of the desert terrain outside the city, two small lakes in the mountains, and a three-and-a-half-mile stretch of the Colorado River. Dealing with the river was especially tricky. Every year, they had to construct fish habitats to boost local populations of trout, whitefish, and bonytail for the upcoming fishing season.

The project started six years ago, when the habitats were made entirely of tubes and pipes. They looked great, but the fish ignored them. That was when Scott had the idea to make the habitats partially from plant matter. He had some old Christmas trees out back, and he thought they'd be put to good use. The fish went nuts. Farber had its best fishing season in years. Who knew that the bonytail's favorite food was old Christmas tree branches?

This year, Scott and his crew had the project down to a science. They each spent an hour piecing the pipes together and wrapping branches around the edges. Then, once Scott checked everyone's handiwork, they sank their new creations to the bottom of the Colorado, clustering them in strategic checkpoints where the targeted fish were known to spawn.

It sounded simple enough—and it was certainly easier than relocating endangered tortoises or trekking through the desert in cooperation with border patrol—but it was still hard work. Quinn had already sweated through his shirt. Everyone else had opted to go shirtless and let their muscled torsos bronze in the sun.

Scott bound more branches together. Three branches down, two more to go. Then he'd be able to chuck this one into the water.

In his head, Scott replayed the events of yesterday. The car ride. The housework. The hug that was more than a hug. It was the first time he and Ramona had been together, just the two of them, in a long time—definitely since the wedding three months ago. There were some phone calls here and there, and a few overlapping visits to the hospital, but nothing like yesterday. They'd laughed together. They'd joked together. He'd even managed to distract her from her motion sickness, though she probably didn't realize he'd noticed. Whatever wall they had built between each other three months ago was officially starting to crumble. It was just ironic that he finally got his old friend back as soon as she started pretending to be somebody else.

But then there was the moment at the house, when she had steadied his shoulders and comforted him. In that moment, he'd needed her. But it was more than just friendship that he needed.

No, it felt intimate. Not like Scott hugging his book-reading, water balloon-throwing next-door neighbor. Ramona was still those things, but yesterday was the first time she'd felt like more than just the neighbor girl. And that was why he told her she could go home. He couldn't handle the confusion. At the time, it felt like the right thing to do. Now, he wasn't so sure.

Because now, no matter how hard he tried, he couldn't get her out of his head.

If he hadn't been thinking so hard, he would've noticed earlier that Miguel had used the wrong knot to bind the corner pieces. More importantly, he would've noticed that Miguel had both feet in the water and was leaning halfway over the side.

"Miguel," Scott said. "We'll swim later. This part of the river is too swift, okay?"

Miguel nodded. He had only been working there a few weeks, but Scott could already tell he was a little reckless. He'd have to keep his eye on him.

As crew leader, it was Scott's job to watch out for the other crewmen and take them to task for any foolish decisions. Normally, he would. Normally, he'd shout, "Miguel! Eyes on the prize!" But he just didn't have it in him to shout. Not today.

Miguel would calm down. Scott knew it.

Sunlight gleamed off the gently rolling waves around them. The Colorado River was always deceptively calm. If anyone looked at the slow, meandering current at its surface, they'd assume the river was gentle and safe. Few people realized how fast the water moved just below the surface.

Miguel leaned over the edge and dipped his head into the water so he could cool off. When he sat back up, his hair was swirled to the side. He was laughing. "Jeez," he said. "I almost fell in."

That was it! No more Mr. Nice Guy. "Miguel," Scott said. "You know the rules."

"C'mon, Scott. I was just—"

"Just nothing," he grumbled. "Get back to work."

Quinn and Terry both glanced at him sideways. Quinn, the oldest of the group, didn't even try to hide it. He just scratched his graying mustache and stared at Scott.

"Back to work," Scott shouted again. To everybody. To himself. The crew scrambled to look busy.

"Dude," Terry said. "Why are you all … wonky?" The California native didn't sound like the rest of his coworkers, who were all born and bred in Arizona. Terry still sounded like he was auditioning to be an extra in *90210*.

No one said anything. Scott certainly didn't answer, because he knew that he would shout again.

To break the awkward silence, Quinn slapped Scott on the back and said, "Hey, congratulations on your mom."

"Yeah!" Miguel agreed. "They did a nice little article on her in the *Farber Daily News*. 'Miracle woman wakes up.' Crazy."

"What?" Terry asked. "Why didn't anyone mention this before? That's, like, major!"

"I don't know," Scott said, not giving any of them eye contact. "It's big news. She's just … not out of the woods yet. I don't know. She's good."

"Then why do you look so distracted?" Quinn asked.

Scott ignored the question. His coworkers knew that he missed his wife, that he was embarrassed by her sudden disappearance, that he—well, that his life was not turning out the way he'd hoped. They knew all of that, so he shouldn't have to keep repeating himself. Besides, he finally wasn't thinking about Nessa. This was a good distracted, not a bad distracted.

Quinn raised his eyebrow. He was in his mid-sixties, and had more life experiences under his belt than the rest of them combined. He knew when something was off. "No!" Quinn shouted. "No, no, no! This isn't about your mom. It's Nessa, isn't it?"

"What?" Miguel asked. He had no idea who Nessa Scapizi was. He'd started working with Scott after the marriage fiasco.

"She came back, didn't she?" Quinn asked, his bushy mustache shaking in the wind. "That's what's got you all messed up!"

"It's not that," Scott said.

"You sure?" Quinn said. "The last time you looked like that … well …"

"She's gone!" Scott shouted. "She's not coming back. It has nothing to do with Nessa."

"But …" Terry said. Everyone knew there was a "but."

"But … her twin sister Ramona is pretending to be her," Scott answered. "At least until Mom is well enough to learn the truth about … everything."

The three guys stared at Scott.

"I thought I could handle it, but … I don't know. It's just weird."

No one said anything for a long time. Then Quinn snorted and Miguel mumbled, "Ay ya," under his breath.

"Dude, that's really freaking weird," Terry said.

Miguel laughed and slapped Scott on the back. "I have no idea what's going on," he said, "but this sounds like one of my mom's *telenovelas*."

Quinn and Terry joined in on the laughter. The only one who remained stone-faced was Scott. He was embarrassed by this whole conversation, and he wished that they could just do their jobs in silence. He hated that Quinn could read him so well, but he hated himself even more for *letting* Quinn read him. Why couldn't he just pull his mind out of the clouds and get back to work?

Pretty soon, all three BLM guys were staring at Scott again.

"Hey, man," Miguel said. "We're joking. You don't have to—"

Quinn cut him off. "You're okay, right?" he said.

Scott looked away.

"Dude!" Terry said. "You can't get hung up on What's-Her-Name. That's just not right."

Miguel nodded. "Yeah. My *abuela* had a saying. Every time she caught me chasing after a girl that was clearly not interested, she would whack me across the head and say, *'Mijo. Eres un estúpido. Piñas que no son las uvas.'*"

"Deep, man," Terry said. "What does that mean?"

Miguel shrugged. "Dunno. Don't speak Spanish. For me, though, it was more about getting whacked in the head. And it worked."

Scott wanted to tell Miguel that he'd probably gotten whacked in the head one too many times, but he didn't want to prolong the conversation. Besides, they were right. Scott was acting very *estúpido*. He didn't love Ramona; he didn't even think of her in those terms. They were friends. That was it. But it didn't change the fact that he was—distracted.

"Guys, I'm fine," Scott finally said. "This Ramona situation will be over in a week or two."

"I hope you're right," Quinn said. "I'd hate to see you get your heart broken by *both* twins."

• • •

Ramona set the last of the decoration boxes onto Debra's bedroom floor. A loud cracking noise came from inside one of the boxes.

I hope that wasn't something valuable, she thought. *Also, I hope Debra didn't hear.*

She'd spent the last half hour hauling these boxes from their dusty corner of the attic. She still had plenty of time before the Welcome Back party, but Debra wanted to get things rolling.

"Thanks so much," Debra said. She probably didn't hear the crack.

"No problem, Debra." Now that the heavy lifting was over, Ramona took the opportunity to gaze around the room. Debra's bedroom was remarkably unchanged: the same duck wallpaper (courtesy of her late husband), the same antique furniture, the same woody smell.

Ramona couldn't remember the last time she'd been up in Debra's room. It must've been years, probably not since third grade, when she and Nessa sneaked in and tried on Debra's old perfume. That was one of the only times she'd ever seen Debra get mad at her. At the time, she swore to herself that she would never make Debra McInney angry again.

Ramona loved this house. There was no other way to say it. She loved this house more than any other place in the world. More than Disneyland. As a kid, this was her haven. Most nights, while her parents were busy shouting and throwing plates, Ramona and her sister came here to escape. The place felt magical and grand, even though it wasn't.

When she was six, Ramona started calling it McInney Manor. Debra liked that name, mostly, she said, because she was so impressed that a six-year-old knew the word "manor." And throughout the years, that name stuck. It had two stories, a grand staircase, and a sprawling yard, but no one would mistake this for a manor. It was a house, a decidedly middle-class house.

But to Ramona—

To Ramona, this was a manor.

She ran her fingertips along the wooden walls. So many memories here.

"Are those the last of the boxes?" Debra asked.

"I think so," Ramona answered. "Should we start going through them?"

Debra sighed. She was a strong woman, and she hated to admit weakness. "Not today," she said. "I think that can wait till tomorrow."

Ramona glanced at the pile of unopened boxes sitting in the middle of the bedroom. Surely there was a better place to keep them. Where they were, anyone could trip over them.

Maybe she should just drag them into the corner of the room. Ramona reached for the closest one.

"Leave them be," Debra ordered. "They can wait till tomorrow."

"Sorry," Ramona mumbled.

"How's your sister?" Debra asked. She always had the amazing ability to change the subject at the drop of a hat.

For one horrifying second, Ramona thought that she was asking about Nessa. *Does she know? Is she testing me?* Then Ramona realized, with a loud gulp, that Debra still thought she was talking to Nessa.

"Ramona?" Ramona said.

"That's the only sister you have," Debra said. "You two were always so much alike. I could never tell you apart."

That's for sure.

Ramona sat on the edge of the bed. "Ramona is … she's fine."

Debra cocked an eyebrow. "You don't sound so sure of that."

"No, no. She's fine. Period. Full stop. She really wants to visit once you get a little better."

Debra smiled. "Tell her anytime. I'm not going anywhere."

"Good to hear," Ramona said.

"And Nessa?" she added. "Don't ever tell her what I told you on your wedding night."

Ramona's heart raced. Her veins jump-roped in her chest. *Don't ever tell her what I told you on your wedding night?* What could Debra possibly have said? What kind of secrets were they keeping from her?

Debra could read the confusion in her face, so she said, "You know, about Scott."

Is it bad? Is this the reason Nessa ran off without saying anything?

"You don't remember, do you?" Debra asked.

"That whole night was such a blur," Ramona answered.

Debra gestured for Ramona to scoot closer. She did.

"Oh, honey," the older woman said. "You were such a bundle of nerves. You needed someone to talk to, and it meant so much that you decided to talk to me. But I thought it was strange that you didn't want to talk to your sister."

"That *was* strange," Ramona said. After all, she was the maid of honor. She was the identical twin, for crying out loud! She should've known that her sister was having cold feet.

"But I knew the reason," Debra said. "Right away, I knew. And I'm going to tell you now what I told you then: Scott made his choice. He loves you. Sure, he has a special place in his heart for Ramona, but you're the one he chose. Ramona is his best friend, but you're his wife. And that's all that matters."

Debra laid it out so plainly. And just like that, Ramona felt the world crash all around her. She'd felt this way when Nessa told her about the engagement. She'd felt this way during the wedding itself. And she felt this way now, when her would-be mother-in-law told her that she was the other one, the unloved one.

This was so much information. She wanted to get it straight. "So *I* told you that I was worried that Scott had feelings for Ramona," she said.

"Yes."

"And that was the reason I was having cold feet?"

"That and the fact that you two had only been dating for a month," Debra said, not in a judgmental way. "Seriously, dear, are you testing my memory or what?"

Ramona didn't want to sound suspicious, so she decided not to ask any more questions. "No. Sorry. And that is good advice," she said. She felt tears well up in her eyes. She smiled, trying to make them seem like happy tears.

"That's my girl," Debra said. "Whatever you do, don't let my son get in the way of your relationship with your sister. Blood is the strongest bond there is. And there's more than enough room in Scott's heart for both of you, the wife and the friend."

"Thanks," Ramona said. "That means a lot."

"I'll see you tomorrow."

Ramona had to concentrate on walking. One foot in front of the other. Repeat. Repeat. Otherwise, she'd trip over those damn boxes, or over her own clumsy feet, and topple down the stairs.

She didn't even bother wiping away the tears.

Deep down, she knew where she stood with Scott. The "Friend Zone," or whatever they call it on television, has very clear signage. "Welcome to the Friend Zone." None of this was new to her. But having Debra, the closest mother figure in her life, lay it out like that—Ramona hurt.

She wanted to make a quick exit. Normally, she'd dawdle in the living room, admiring the woodwork and appreciating the family photos. Normally, she'd linger. But suddenly this house didn't seem as inviting. It seemed oppressive.

What was worse, she didn't feel like a part of the house. Not anymore. As a kid, McInney Manor felt like her real home. Here, no one screamed at each other. No one threw plates. Even though it was just wood, and concrete, and plaster, the house always called out to her. It was the X on her pirate map.

But now—now she didn't know how she felt, except for the nagging feeling that she had to leave. Right away.

When she got to the bottom of the stairs, she looked around to see if anyone else was here. She didn't need any more conversation, at least not now. The coast was clear, so Ramona spy-walked through the empty hallway and the empty kitchen. All she had to do was cross the living room. Then she'd make her escape.

But as she entered the living room, she heard a horrible cry of pain. Then another. Then another. Then a gruff voice barked, "Over here, soldiers!"

Great. Someone was watching TV.

No, that wasn't quite right. Someone was playing a video game.

Ramona saw a blond mop of hair peeking out over the top of the couch: Jeffrey. His back was to her. She could see that he was blasting some sort of green creatures with a laser gun.

He seemed completely invested in his mission. Maybe he wouldn't notice her leaving.

Ramona knew every inch of this house, but she seemed to always forget that one inch—that one very important inch of floorboard that creaked every time someone stepped on it.

Creeeeeaaak.

"Ramona?" Jeffrey asked without turning.

"Yeah," she admitted. "I was just—"

"Ramona, can I ask you something?" He still didn't turn to look at her.

"Sure?"

"Dad always tells me that lying is bad," he said. "You know, like about grades and stuff."

"Your father is a very wise man," Ramona said.

"Don't flatter him," Jeffrey corrected. "Everyone knows that lying is bad. Especially when you lie to old people. That's like the worst."

He killed a few more creatures.

Ramona had the sinking suspicion that she knew where this conversation was headed. "Honey," she said. "I really have to get going. I'm late for—"

"Why are you lying to Grandma?" the boy blurted out.

Such a simple question. Such a simple, simple question.

"Well," Ramona said, "your grandma is still sick. And we thought that it would help her get better if we—"

"If you pretended to be Aunt Nessa?"

"Did your daddy tell you that?" Ramona asked.

"Yeah."

"It's true," she said. She couldn't lie to him.

He didn't say anything for a long time. The only sounds in that living room were floor creaks and video game death noises. Ramona thought she was finally in the clear, but then Jeffrey said, "Why?"

Ramona smiled down at Jeffrey, but he didn't notice. He was too busy killing space mutants. Or zombies.

"You know what, Jeffrey?" she said. She looked at the TV screen. Yup. Definitely space mutants.

"What?" the boy asked.

"I honestly don't know."

Chapter Six

Ramona grabbed two packets of organic, wheat-based cracker substitutes, and tossed them into her cart. There was a little alligator logo on the covers, which meant that the food company spent a percentage of its profits protecting the Florida wetland.

Or something.

Ramona never bothered reading the description, but she knew it was good for the environment. She also knew these snacks would be good for Debra's recovery. They weren't exactly what she had written on the shopping list, but they also weren't jam-packed with butter and high-fructose corn syrup, either. Ramona tasked herself with making sure Debra ate right, even if that meant a few moments of grocery-unpacking disappointment.

Her cell phone buzzed in her pocket. Three warning buzzes and then her ringtone: the default classical music that came with this model. She'd had the phone for a year and a half, yet she hadn't bothered to change the music to something she liked.

Or at least something that didn't actively make her teeth chatter.

Her teeth chattered.

She knew it wasn't work, because she'd already told Nancy that she'd be running errands all day. Plus, the latest shipment of paperbacks wasn't expected till Friday.

No, this wasn't business. This had to be pleasure.

She looked at the screen. Scott's name popped up. *Great,* she thought. Scott McInney, the worst kind of pleasure.

"Hello?"

"Whatcha doing?" Scott asked. God, he knew she hated that.

For a second, Ramona wondered if she should lie about shopping. If he knew where she was, he'd probably make a couple of requests too, probably of the butter and high-fructose corn syrup variety.

Then she realized that was stupid. She was a grown woman; she could always tell him no.

"I'm at the supermarket," she said. "Your mom needed some supplies."

"You should get her some good, old-fashioned junk food," he suggested. "It'll be a nice change of pace from, well, from getting nutrients through an IV."

"No junk food." Ramona needed to put her foot down then and there. If not, then this would quickly escalate into a high-stakes negotiation. *I'll trade you the soy milk for the boxed mac and cheese, but only if you upgrade the fat-free cream cheese to reduced-fat and jalapeno-flavored.*

"Come on," Scott bargained. "Just one box of—"

"Nope." Suddenly, she was reminded of the hours they spend in their treehouse as kids. He'd always steal her Barbies, just so they could play Hostage Negotiator. It was fun, even if things didn't always end so well for Barbie.

"You know, a little junk food can be good for her."

"That's not true."

"It is! Happy taste buds equal happy lives. Haven't you ever heard that saying?"

"I'm pretty sure you just made that up."

"Yeah. I did."

"Okay. Fine," she gave in. "We can get her one thing from the bad list. What would you say is her favorite?"

Without thinking, he said, "Those maple cookies. The ones with the Amish lady on the front."

Ramona was standing in the crackers aisle, so she could clearly see the cookies he was talking about. She also knew that the mascot was just a regular, old, non-Amish grandmother, but she wasn't going to start another argument.

She placed her hand on the box, but then pulled away. Scott wasn't even in the same room as her, yet he was still calling the shots. If she was going to remain sane for the next week or so, she needed to reassert herself.

"I just grabbed one box," she lied.

Scott paused for a few seconds. "No, you didn't," he said.

"What?"

"You didn't grab any cookies. Come on. They're right by your elbow."

Ramona spun around. Yup, there he was, casually leaning against a rack of discount tortillas. He had a phone in one hand and barbecue ranch potato chips in the other. He always ate such disgusting snacks. It was a real testament to his outdoorsy lifestyle that he could keep in such good shape.

He clicked off his phone.

"You were spying on me," she said. Not a question.

"A little." He walked over to her and tossed a box of maple cookies into her cart. "Come on. Don't look at me like that. I was just calling you to see if we needed milk back at the house. I didn't realize you were shopping, too. And I also didn't realize that you were in the same store until I saw you in the cookie aisle. Lying to me, I might add."

She didn't know if she should be embarrassed or mad or happy to see him. She chose D: none of the above.

Scott glanced at the piles of health food in her cart. "You trying to kill us?" he asked.

She could explain to him about the importance of a nutrient-rich diet, or about saving the Florida wetlands, but she knew she couldn't change the mind of someone whose idea of lunch was half a bag of barbecue ranch potato chips. Instead, she told him, "This is the food Dr. Nguyen recommended." He could argue with her all he wanted, but he couldn't argue with a licensed medical professional.

"Those were suggestions," Scott said.

Well, maybe he could argue with anything.

"Exactly," Ramona said. "And that's why we're getting one box of maple cookies."

"Jeez, Ramona. I expected more from you. I mean, I knew you were always the health nut, but—"

"What's wrong with being healthy?"

"The better question is, 'What's wrong with eating cardboard?' And the answer: everything," he said. "Naw, you were always the organic soy militant, and Nessa was always sneaking me the good stuff." He held up his potato chips for evidence.

Ramona bristled at her sister's name. So few people mentioned Nessa these days, that when she did hear it, a bunch of negative images flashed into her head.

"Hey, sorry," Scott said. "I didn't mean to … I know it's still a sore subject."

"Naw. It's not your fault." But even though the words came out of her mouth, and even though she wanted to believe she was over it—

She started walking away.

"Wait."

"I really have to finish these errands," she said. "I should've been back at the house a half hour ago." She walked faster and faster down the cookie aisle, until she found herself practically jogging behind her shopping cart.

He chased after her. She hadn't gotten far, just a few feet past the cereals. "Wait. I'm, well, I'm sorry for bringing up Nessa. I know it's a sore subject."

"Look," she said. "I'm not mad." And she certainly wasn't. She was sad. She was the other sister, the one not chosen, and that didn't make her angry—except maybe at herself.

"I don't buy that for a second," he said.

"I'm not!"

"Ramona, come on. This is me you're talking to. I know when you're mad. Believe me." He said it like she was constantly in a state of anger, like she was Grumpy Smurf or something.

To prove that he was wrong, to prove that he didn't know the first thing about Ramona Scapizi, she said, "Scott, would you like to help me finish the rest of my list?"

"I would love to."

Together, they walked to the bakery aisle.

• • •

Scott was already late for work. His lunch break had already started to bleed into his afternoon. As soon as he helped Ramona load up these groceries into her van, then he'd be off.

Just his luck, had Ramona decided to park all the way on the other side of the parking lot. "It's good to walk," she always said.

Every time Scott saw Ramona's wheels—a light brown van at least a decade past its prime—he couldn't help thinking that she drove the dorkiest vehicle on the planet. It was a van meant for soccer moms, not unmarried twentysomethings who should know better.

Then again, she'd had it forever. It was almost like her trademark. He couldn't picture her driving a little pink sports car.

Scott grabbed the last bag from the cart. *All that damn health food*, he thought. *It just wasn't natural.*

Then again, the green apples looked pretty delicious. Maybe if he just grabbed one—

When Ramona's back was turned, he sneaked the biggest, juiciest-looking apple from the bag. He couldn't tell if she'd seen him from the corner of her eye.

He took a big bite, letting the flavors dance across his taste buds. Definitely better than barbecue ranch potato chips.

Ramona grabbed the bag from Scott's hand. "Funny," she said. "It feels a little lighter than it did before."

Scott smiled. His mouth was closed, of course.

"It's almost like … naw, it couldn't be," Ramona continued. "Then again … it's almost like something's gone missing."

Scott hid the apple behind his back.

"You sure you didn't steal anything?" she asked.

"I would never," Scott answered, but his mouth was full of apple at the time. He smiled like a kid with his hand in the cookie jar.

She didn't say anything for a long moment. Then she held out her hand. Scott gave her the apple. It was big and green, perfect except for the single bite mark.

Then she took a bite.

Scott couldn't help but stare as at least three separate reactions played across Ramona's face.

1) Surprise, as if she hadn't expected the apple to be this tart.

2) Determination, as if she wouldn't give Scott the satisfaction of seeing her face scrunch up like a baby eating a lemon for the first time.

3) Enjoyment. Tart or not, it tasted good.

"Thanks," she said when her mouth was no longer full.

Scott felt that undeniable feeling in the pit of his stomach—that feeling he felt when she'd held him yesterday—that *Ramona* feeling. There was no other way to put it. She brought something out of him that he could never put into words, especially not to her.

If he was honest with himself, it was the same feeling she'd always given him, only more intense now. And if he was *really* being honest with himself, he knew that feeling, that unnamable feeling, was the real reason he'd never dated Ramona. He knew that if he put himself out there and tried to push things too far, he could lose her—and that feeling—forever.

Even more, that feeling was also why he started dating Nessa. She was his friend, too, but they weren't nearly as close. Their connection wasn't as strong. It was a safer place for a romantic relationship to start. And everything seemed to work out okay— until Nessa disappeared.

"What's with the face?" Ramona asked.

Crap. She'd caught him. "What face?"

"Nothing," she said, but her tone of voice implied that there was definitely more than nothing.

Scott quickly made his face go blank. He wasn't much of a poker player, but he did have a knack for hiding his expression when he was bluffing—or when he wasn't.

One thing was clear. He knew he had to sort out these feelings. If he didn't, she wouldn't be in his life at all. Not as a friend, or anything else.

I have to talk to her about this, he thought.

Bam! Ramona slammed the trunk shut. The sudden noise jarred him back to reality.

Just not right now.

•••

After hours of digging irrigation canals in the hot desert sun, all Scott wanted to do was take a shower and watch football. Heck, he'd be happy to sit through a soap-opera marathon if it meant sitting on a sofa inside an air-conditioned building.

While visions of basic cable danced in his head, Scott walked back toward the dune buggy he'd parked a few feet away.

"Dude!" Terry called from a few yards back.

Scott quickened his pace. Even though Terry was one of his closest friends—despite the surfer dude loopiness and the constant marijuana haze—he didn't feel very sociable right now. Let him bum a ride from Quinn and Miguel. Their Jeep was just down the hill.

"Yo! Scott-ay!" Terry called again, louder than before.

Scott paused next to the dune buggy. It was no use ignoring him. Terry would follow him to the ends of the earth, for better or worse. "Hey, man," Scott said. "Hop on in. I'll take you back." The invitation was more of a formality than anything. Terry was already mid-hop before the words even left Scott's mouth.

In a few seconds, Scott had revved the engine and begun his slow, careful drive down the mountainside.

"Dude," Terry said, "you know you can go a little faster. I'm not exactly precious cargo."

Scott's grip on the steering wheel tightened.

"Hot day, huh?" Terry tried for some more small talk. "I think I lost like twenty pounds in sweat."

"Then you'd be dead," Scott muttered. He was in no mood for small talk.

"Dude. It's called hyperbole. Jeez. All I'm sayin' is it's hot today."

Because there was no windshield on the dune buggy, hot wind blasted their faces and pelted them with sand. Scott wanted to get inside—*needed* to get inside—as quickly as possible.

"Agreed."

"Dude, what's with you? You still all funked out over Ramona?"

"Naw," he lied. "I'm just … okay, yeah. I didn't expect to be seeing her all the time. It's like, since she agreed to pretend to be Nessa, she's just always around. She helps my mom, which is great. But she also, I don't know …"

"You don't want her around?"

The dune buggy sped up. Scott didn't realize his foot pressed down so hard on the gas. The wind got hotter.

"No," he said. "I do. In fact, I love seeing her … you know, helping Mom and stuff."

"You're worried that you like it too much," Terry guessed. For someone with sun-bleached highlights and an eyebrow piercing, Terry was surprisingly insightful.

Scott couldn't admit that, though. "Not at all," he said.

"Well, whatever you're feeling, you need to go and talk with her."

"I do," he said.

"On her terms," Terry said. "Go to her work or something. Have lunch. Just hash things out, friend to friend."

"Okay."

They were roaring down the hill now. Scott never drove this fast, at least not when he was paying attention.

"You know what? Maybe. I'm a total idiot, right?"

Terry didn't agree. Instead, he shouted, "Look out!"

The BLM office was in front of them, and it was coming up fast. Scott slammed his foot on the brake. The dune buggy lurched to a stop, its back tires rising into the air. For an awful second, Scott felt like the entire vehicle was going to cartwheel forward, landing upside-down in the rock-peppered sand.

But the back wheels came back down, slamming into the ground and shooting dirt in all directions. Scott coughed up a lungful of desert.

"Sorry, man," Scott said. "I guess I wasn't paying attention to the odometer."

Terry jumped out of the vehicle, landing on wobbly legs.

"It's okay, dude," he said. "But next time, I'll probably hitch a ride with Quinn and Miguel instead."

Chapter Seven

As Scott approached the big stone lions outside the library building, he felt a wave of self-doubt. This was a bad idea. He shouldn't surprise Ramona at work. She'd read too much into it.

He knew he needed to talk to her, to thank her for everything she was doing—and everything she was going to do—for him and his family. And he needed to explain exactly what she meant to him.

No.

He couldn't. Not at her work. Not face to face.

Maybe he could just call her tonight. He was already asking too much of her. He'd already fake-proposed to her in front of the sick and wounded.

Why was he acting like such a chicken? His job was full of dangers and pitfalls. He constantly charged into difficult situations. Why did this stupid library make his pulse go all jittery?

He couldn't do it. He turned to leave.

"Scott?" a familiar voice called to him.

Crap.

He spun around. "Ramona. Hi. Crazy meeting you here."

"At my work?" she said.

"Oh, you work here? I completely forgot." Scott had a weird tendency to avoid an awkward situation by instantly dialing up the awkwardness and turning everything into a big joke.

"So are you interested in the new releases?" she asked.

She was glad to see him; he could tell. She crinkled her nose when she smiled. He hadn't seen her do that in forever, not since before his engagement. That one little expression calmed all his nerves.

"Actually, I wanted to ask you if you wanted to go to lunch," he said. "But I don't know. You look busy." He gestured toward the stack of books in her hand. "Maybe another time?"

Ramona dropped all the books onto the nearest shelf. "I'm ready," she said, looking ready to charge into battle. She might as well have cocked a rifle and said, "It's game time."

After a moment of lunch negotiations, they both agreed to eat at the trendy new place across the street. It used to be a deli they both liked, but had been remodeled in the last year to cater to high-end customers. Hopefully, the food would be as good as it used to be.

The restaurant was trendy, which meant expensive and busy and filled with abstract art. Their waiter tossed some menus onto the table. Apparently, "trendy" also meant rude. Before they could open the menus, the waiter asked, "Know what you want?"

"Hmm," Scott said. "I'll have—"

Ramona cut him off. "He'll have the clam chowder and coffee. I know it's kind of a weird combo, especially in hot weather like this, but don't judge him."

"You remembered!" Scott said. He was impressed, but not entirely surprised.

"Of course. It's just so weird."

The waiter forced a smile, but Scott could tell he wanted to move on to the next table. "And for you, ma'am?"

Ramona looked at him, her eyes daring him to order for her.

He knew what she wanted, of course: egg salad on sourdough. Always egg salad. As long as there wasn't too much mayo, she was happy.

But did he really want to show her how much he knew about her? It seemed like that would cross some sort of friend/boyfriend line, and he wasn't ready to cross that.

Whatever. He might as well just order the egg salad. That was her favorite.

"Well?" the waiter asked.

"Roast beef."

Ramona's expression went blank. She was always so good at hiding her disappointment, but Scott could see it—every bit of that disappointment—in the edges of her lips.

Scott looked away.

"My favorite," Ramona told the waiter.

He quickly wrote down their orders and disappeared into the kitchen.

"So what did you want to talk about?" she asked. All business, as always.

"I just wanted to have lunch."

"But your mom's not here."

"I know." He paused for a moment. He should've ordered her egg salad. That was what she really wanted. "Here's the thing. If we're going to get along, there's something I need to tell you."

She looked hopeful. But hopeful for what, exactly?

"I just wanted you to know," he started. "I mean, the last couple of days have been a little confusing, but I just wanted you to know that if I crossed any sort of boundary with you—"

"You didn't."

"If I did, I'm sorry," he said. Words weren't coming out right.

"What are you trying to say?" she asked.

"Um," he said. If this made-up relationship would ever work, and if he was going to continue having Ramona in his life, he needed to be honest with her. "Things have been weird between us for a long time. I started dating your sister, and it was like a switch turned off. You … kept your distance. And I spent my time with her. And then when the wedding happened—"

"It was so fast."

"Yeah," he admitted. "It was. And things got even weirder between us after the wedding. I feel like we're finally getting back on track. As friends."

"As friends," she repeated.

Light streamed in through the restaurant windows, dancing across the loose curls of Ramona's hair. Her hair glowed with oranges and yellows. Sunlight was different in Arizona, brighter somehow. He knew it firsthand from working outside in the desert. And he knew it right now, looking at the soft curve of her cheek, the glow in her eye. Arizona sun was different. And it looked good on her.

The waiter came back with their food and refilled both their waters. Ramona looked at her sandwich for a second, just a second, and said, "Well, at least it doesn't have mayonnaise. You know how I hate that."

"Thank you," he said.

She looked at him funny.

"For being there for me," he said.

"It's not that hard," she said. "I care so much about your mom. I kind of have to help out, you know?"

"Not just this. Not just now." He flicked at his straw. "I mean, always. You've always been there for me. So … thanks."

"You're welcome."

"One of the hardest things about the last couple of months was that I couldn't talk to you about any of it."

"You could've called me."

"And talked to you about your sister? I couldn't. Things were complicated enough. And when she ran off, I knew I couldn't vent my feelings with you."

"You could've."

"Stop saying that. You know it's not true."

"You're probably right," she said.

Their food was getting cold really quickly.

"But now," he continued, "it's just good to have you back in my life again." He leaned forward and placed his hand on hers. "It's good to have you back."

He had to play it safe. He couldn't lose her again. He wanted to kiss her—oh, God, he wanted to kiss her—but he knew that if he did—

Things would change.

Things would go bad.

Just like what happened with Nessa.

"As a friend," he said. As the words came out of his mouth, they hurt. They caused him actual pain. But in his mind, he knew that he'd done the right thing.

"Okay," she said. And this time, he couldn't read her expression.

• • •

"Can you help me with these cans?" Debra asked. The doctor had told her not to exert herself, yet there she was, standing on her tiptoes with several cans of soup in each hand.

"Stop," Ramona nagged. "I told you I can put everything away. You're too—"

"I'm too what, dear?"

"Short," Ramona answered. "You're too short to put these away. I've got a good two inches on you."

Debra handed her the cans and pointed toward their destination, the top shelf on the right. "Nice save, dear."

The back door creaked open. Ramona looked up just in time to see Scott McInney, his muscular arms full of groceries, walk into the kitchen. He had a smile on his face, at least until he saw his fake-wife leaning against the counter. A shadow passed over his face, and his expression morphed from carefree to businesslike.

Every time he entered a room, Ramona's brain stopped and started, like a computer screen blinking on and off. He was her virus, her glitch in the system.

And God, what a glitch. He still wore his BLM shirt, which was at least a size too tight. It clung to his body, smudged and sweat-stained, and the wide expanse of his shoulders and arms flexed underneath.

"Hello, ladies," he said.

Ramona could've kicked herself. He wasn't supposed to see her staring at him like a piece of meat. It was too embarrassing, especially after their lunch date yesterday. He had made everything abundantly clear: He wanted to be friends.

Friends.

"Stop right there," Debra demanded. And when Debra demanded something, you obeyed. "That's no way to treat your new wife."

"No, it's not," Ramona added playfully. Her cheeks blushed pink.

"Long day at work," he mumbled, but that wasn't good enough for his mother.

"All the more reason to appreciate Nessa," she said. Except for the "Nessa" part, Ramona liked where this conversation was headed.

"Kiss her, Scott," Debra said. "Your father kissed me every chance he got. And look at me now."

A few days ago, that would've been a joke. But now, after two days of walking and talking and giving orders, she was starting to look like herself again. Her coloring wasn't 100 percent yet, and she was still too skinny, but she didn't move with the same creakiness that she had when she'd first woken up.

"You do look lovely," Ramona offered.

"Thanks, dear. Now please kiss your husband before I think ill of you."

Ramona and Scott exchanged glances. They didn't have a choice. Ramona waited for Scott to make the first move, and when he didn't, she wrapped her arms around him and planted her lips on his.

Right away, she felt a jolt of contact, as his soft lips brushed lightly against hers. Then her lips parted, and his tongue slid into her mouth, tasting her for the first time. She certainly hadn't expected that.

It was too late to turn back now, so she returned the favor. Her tongue guided his, feeling its warmth and taking control. She was kissing on her own terms. She grabbed the back of his neck and guided his head to the left. She wrapped her other arm around his trim waist.

That was way too good to be a kiss of friendship.

She pulled away. And when she did, she saw him staring at her, speechless and almost out of breath.

"See?" Debra said. "That wasn't too hard, now, was it?"

"No, ma'am," Scott answered his mom, but he was still staring at Ramona.

"It certainly didn't look that way," Debra said. "In fact, I'm surprised you've already been married for three months, considering how you kiss like newlyweds."

Feeling bold after that moment of sudden passion, Ramona wrapped her arm around his shoulder. "We're just deeply in love, that's all," she said.

Scott accidentally knocked one of the grocery bags onto the floor. A single orange rolled around the linoleum in a wide circle. After all that hemming and hawing from the other day, he'd actually bought something nutritious.

"Of course," Debra said. "Listen, why don't you two go out to the garden and spend some time together?"

Ramona gulped. She felt emboldened, but not *that* emboldened. A quick kiss was one thing—especially since they were put on the spot like that—but Debra wanted them to have some serious alone time together, and Ramona didn't feel ready for that yet.

Judging by Scott's expression, he felt the same way.

"But ..." Ramona said.

"But we should help you put everything away," Scott added. Good save!

Debra placed her hands on his chest and pushed him toward the door. "Nonsense," she said. "I can get Rob to do that for me. He didn't work today, remember?"

"Right."

Now they didn't have an excuse. None at all.

Ramona and Scott exchanged another look, this one of surrender. They took each other's hands and walked outside.

Because Ramona wasn't entirely made of stone, she got shivers from the gentle pressure that Scott placed on her hand. His hand was so much bigger than hers. Rougher, too. He held her, firm but not too firm. From this simple bit of contact, she knew his strength.

They entered the garden.

Since Debra had her accident, their three-acre plot of land had turned wild and overgrown. It needed Debra's near-constant groundskeeping, and without her, grass sprouted up through cracks in stone and weeds mingled with the flowers. Surely, Scott could've maintained it while Debra was sick, but somehow he didn't.

"It's changed a lot," Ramona said. "The garden, I mean."

Scott nodded, but didn't answer.

"We should probably spruce it up before the party," she continued.

"I'm sure Rob can help you with that," Scott said. "I keep encouraging him to go outside more."

Ramona wanted to ask him why he wouldn't fix up the yard. He was a park ranger, after all; out of everyone in the McInney family, he was by far the most qualified. But she didn't want to offend him, so they walked together in silence.

Eventually, Ramona realized that Scott was taking her directly toward his old treehouse, a small wooden structure built in one of the highest trees in the yard. Even though she was an adult now, it still amazed her that Scott's family had been able to build such a big room way up in the branches.

She did notice, however, that some of the boards were broken and the curtain had fallen off. Even the ladder looked like it was about to crumble in two.

"It's … um, seen better days," Scott admitted.

"It certainly has," Ramona agreed, her mind drifting back to some of those *better days*. If she squinted hard enough, she could see little Scott McInney pulling himself up the tattered rope hanging from its window. She saw herself leaning out the window, shouting, "Come on, Scott. Faster. Faster!" She saw Scott get momentarily distracted, his eight-year-old body tensing, before he lost his grip and fell all the way to the ground.

He'd come a long way since then.

"Remember when you fell from that rope?" Ramona asked.

"'Course I do," he admitted. "You bet me I couldn't climb all the way to the top."

"And guess what?" she said. "You didn't."

"Yeah, well, I still blame you for that. I don't think my tailbone ever healed completely."

She nudged him playfully. "Shut up. You told me you didn't feel anything."

Scott placed his large hands on the rough bark of the tree. He looked like he was reliving the memory. "Of course that's what I said. I was a kid. I didn't want to embarrass myself."

"So it really hurt?"

"Like hell," he admitted. "I wasn't going to tell you that. I also wasn't going to mention that I landed on a pine cone."

"Ouch."

"But hey, now that we're back here, I think it's time that you honor your part of the deal." A devilish smile spread across Scott's face, and Ramona knew she wasn't going to like what he was about to propose.

"And what deal is that?" he asked.

"We were both supposed to climb that rope," he explained. "But after I fell and permanently damaged my coccyx, you conveniently forgot that part. I think it's only fair that you follow through on your agreement."

"Meaning—?"

"Meaning, start climbing."

He was serious! Ramona couldn't believe it.

Ramona grabbed hold of the bottom of the rope and looked up. It wound its way around one of the top branches, about twenty feet up. How could they possibly have thought this was a good idea as eight-year-olds? "Naw," she said. "I'm good."

Scott didn't take no for an answer. He grabbed her around the waist and raised her a few feet into the air. "Grab hold," he said. "I'm not gonna let go until you grab hold."

Reluctantly, she wrapped her arms around the dusty rope. The branch above them groaned audibly. She felt dizzy already.

"You still do yoga, right?" Scott asked.

"Uh-huh," Ramona muttered. Twice a week.

"Then you'll have no problem hoisting yourself up. I'll be down here, watching."

Slowly, she reached forward and began to pull herself up. First one hand, then the other. The rope shook underneath her. "What am I doing?" she muttered to herself.

Before she knew it, Ramona was a good six feet over the ground, high enough to feel queasy. This was about the halfway point: *halfway to the treehouse, halfway to a horrible, splattery death,* she thought darkly.

"Wow," Scott said. "I didn't really think you'd—"

"What?" she shouted, clinging as tightly as the Jaws of Life. "You didn't think you could peer pressure me into doing this? Well, ya did. So, congrats!"

He didn't respond, so she glanced down at his expression. Big mistake. The minute her eyes caught the ground far below her, her head started to spin and she felt the rope twisting underneath her like a snake.

She lost her grip.

For one horrible second, the world blurred into colors and she felt her body whoosh through the air. It wasn't long enough for her life to flash before her eyes, but it was long enough for a single horrible thought to cross her mind: *I'm going to die, and it's all Scott McInney's fault.*

She landed with a thump in his strong, outstretched arms. He held her close, waiting for her to catch her breath.

"See?" she said. "Falling wasn't so bad after all."

"That's because you had someone to catch you," Scott said. "The only thing that caught me was a pine cone. And, um, you're welcome, by the way."

She lay in his grip, feeling the hard surfaces of his chest and arms. She could've stayed there forever. She looked into his eyes, which were crinkled and narrowed onto hers.

"I think my mom's watching us from her window," he said.

"So what do you suppose we do about that?" she asked.

In response, he leaned forward and kissed her. Or, at least, he tried to.

And Ramona was certainly tempted.

Even though his face was so close to hers, she couldn't see him clearly. The sun was directly behind him. All she saw was the halo around him, the golden outline that framed every curve of his face. She felt the press of his lips even before it happened. She wanted to feel the press of his lips—

But she couldn't.

At the last second, Ramona jumped out of his strong arms and tumbled onto the ground. "Sorry," she said.

"I'm sorry," he countered. "I was just putting on a show. I should've asked."

"Yeah, you should've." But Ramona didn't really mean that. She liked the way he took charge; she liked a guy who could catch her when she fell. No, it wasn't his fault that she pulled away; it was her own.

Ramona glanced up at Debra's window. The curtains were drawn. She was no longer watching them. They could actually be themselves now, whatever that meant.

Scott stepped a few paces back, trying to get a full view of the treehouse looming above them. He smiled in a far-off kind of way.

"You're not mad at me?" she asked.

Her words pulled him back to reality. "What? Uh, no. I was … just thinking about … everything. We had so many memories up there."

"I know," Ramona said. "Remember how you'd tell those ghost stories? I never got scared, but Nessa …" The instant she mentioned her sister's name, she wished she could take it back. They were having so much fun together—they were so *comfortable* together—and she'd just ruined it by mentioning the one person who'd messed up their lives.

"Maybe we should go back inside," Scott said. He turned toward the house without waiting for a response.

Ramona wasn't ready to go inside, though. Now that she'd mentioned Nessa's name, she had to press the conversation. She just had to. No matter how much Scott hated talking about it, Ramona just had to know. They had gotten so much out in the open during their lunch conversation yesterday, but there was still one answer that Ramona needed. "Um, Scott?" she said.

He didn't turn around. He probably sensed where this conversation was headed.

"About Nessa …"

Scott turned to face her, slowly, calmly. His face was blank. "There's nothing to say. I—"

"Do you regret it?" she asked.

"What?"

"Do you regret marrying her?"

He didn't seem to have an answer, and for one tense moment, Ramona thought he was going to avoid the question. *Just say it,* she thought. *Please. Just tell me how you felt.*

She needed him to say something, anything.

Finally, he looked her right in the eyes and said, "Sometimes."

"Do you love her?" she asked.

"I did."

•••

In a way, it was good that Ramona didn't dream, because if she had, she would've dreamed about Scott.

Instead, she watched late-night infomercials and drank hot cocoa. Debra always told her that cocoa would keep her awake at night, but she was already awake. Wide awake. It couldn't do any more damage. Besides, at least she got to learn about an amazing new vacuum cleaner that also doubled as a mop.

The digital clock on the wall said three twenty-seven. She'd have to be up and ready for work in three hours.

She looked at her cell phone on the end table. She thought about calling Scott. It was a stupid idea for three reasons: A) He wasn't going to be awake at three in the morning, especially not after a long day hauling branches and building fish habitats. B) Her phone call would probably wake up Debra. And C) She certainly didn't want him knowing that she was thinking about him in the middle of the night.

Sure, she used to call him at all hours of the day or night, just to talk (or complain). And he was always more than happy to listen (or pretend to). But it didn't feel right anymore.

Stop thinking about him, she told herself. *Stop it!* But the more she tried to pay attention to the flickering images on the screen—Look! It's a vacuum! Look! It's a mop!—the more she thought about falling into his arms. It felt so natural, just the two of them, together.

Why did he have to love Nessa? Sure, he'd used past tense. He *did* love her. But that was more about his broken heart than an active change in his emotions. He loved her sister, and there was nothing Ramona could do about it.

Yeah, it was probably a good thing that Ramona couldn't sleep, because if she did, she'd dream about Scott. And if she dreamed about Scott, it would very quickly turn into a nightmare.

• • •

Scott woke up in a puddle of sweat. He could barely catch his breath. His clock said it was after three.

Because he had woken up so suddenly, he couldn't remember anything about his dream. All he could remember was the way it made him feel: scared, confused, achy. Was it a dream or a nightmare? He couldn't tell.

Okay, he told himself. *No big deal. Whatever it was …*

But the more he thought about it, the more he realized that this wasn't a nightmare. It was definitely a dream. And even though he felt scared and confused and achy, he knew it had been a good one.

So why had he woken up in a cold sweat? What could he possibly have been dreaming about?

"Scott?" Debra whispered. She stood at his doorway. Her body leaned against the doorframe, merely a silhouette against the hall lights behind her.

The moment he saw his mother's darkened frame, Scott realized that she had been in his dream.

And Ramona was in it, too.

He and Ramona were up in the treehouse, just like when they were kids, and they were doing—something. He couldn't remember. And then Debra saw them. And then he woke up.

Scott wished he could remember everything, but those images were gone now, shaken out of his brain by such a sudden wake-up.

"Scott?" his mother whispered again.

"Uh, yeah. Come in."

She walked inside. It was still too dark to see her face clearly. "I heard something," she said.

"Mom, you're supposed to be sleeping."

Debra sat on the edge of the mattress. She placed her hand on his knee. "I've slept for months," she said. "I've done my time."

That was her excuse for everything, though. Sure, she'd been in a coma, but now was the time for her to heal. Scott couldn't stand to watch her putter around the house like that. She looked like a zombie. He needed her to heal as quickly as possible. He needed his old mom back.

And also—

A dark thought ran through his brain. He didn't want his mom to heal just for her own benefit; he wanted her to heal so that he could finally tell her the truth about Nessa. He wanted his mother to get better for his own damn benefit, too.

He knew it was selfish. But he couldn't stop himself. He wanted Debra to wake up refreshed and healthy and 100-percent rejuvenated, because then he would be free from this fake marriage and all the confusing feelings it inspired.

"I know you're glad to be awake," he said, "but don't you think your body should be back on a normal sleeping schedule?"

"Oh, pooh," she answered, which was as close as she ever got to screaming out obscenities.

Scott studied his mother in the dim light. She had bed-head, which was understandable. Her skin was still pale, but her cheeks had a slight blush of pink, as if color was finally starting to reenter her life. The wrinkles around her eyes were pronounced and deep, but she was also starting to get a few laugh lines around her mouth. She didn't look healthy, but she was getting there.

When she didn't leave, Scott asked, "Is something bugging you?"

"I'm worried about you," she said.

Scott laughed. "You?" he said. "You're worried about me?"

"You were talking in your sleep again."

Scott's whole body went numb. He hadn't talked in his sleep since he was a kid. And even then, it was only when he was stressed or confused about something. What if he'd said something about Ramona and Nessa? What if his mom overheard everything?

"What did you hear?" he asked. Panic flashed across his face.

Debra raised an eyebrow, as if she suspected something but didn't want to say it out loud. "I couldn't make out the words," she said. "It was mostly mumbling. But you certainly sounded anxious."

He still wasn't completely sure if she was telling him the whole story, but there wasn't anything he could do about that now. "I am anxious," he said. "About you. About your recovery."

She patted him on the knee again. "Go back to sleep," she said. "You need your beauty rest."

Chapter Eight

The pepperoni pizza smelled delicious. The anchovy pizza, not so much. But hey, it was Jeffrey's favorite.

Ramona passed Scott the box of garlic bread. She could read his mind.

"Shouldn't we wait for Dad?" Jeffrey asked.

"He's going to be at work for a while," Debra explained. "He's already taken too much time off for my benefit." What Debra didn't know was that Rob's company was really struggling. He'd recently had to lay off a few of his employees, and now he was struggling to do their work on top of his own.

Debra couldn't find out any of that, though. Her heart.

Scott took a huge bite of the pepperoni pizza. It tasted as good as it smelled. "Good choice, Mom," he said.

"I called in the order!" Jeffrey bragged.

Ramona chewed happily. She was leaning forward with her elbows on the table. In other words, she was sitting like Ramona, not Nessa. Nessa always ate her pizza with a fork, too.

Aside from table manners, though, Scott was surprised—and impressed—by how easily Ramona took to the fake-wife act. She walked a little differently. Her speaking voice was a little slower and quieter. All in all, she was a more-than-passable Nessa.

He missed the old her, though. Little moments like these really brought things back into perspective.

He almost didn't want to say anything, but he knew they had to keep up appearances, so he nudged her under the table.

She understood the signal. Right away, she sat up straight and grabbed her silverware.

Scott was halfway done with his first piece before he noticed that Debra wasn't eating. Instead, she sat with her arms in her lap and waited.

"Mom?" he asked.

"Aren't you hungry?" Jeffrey asked. He had tomato sauce on his chin and forehead.

"I'm just taking a moment to appreciate everything." She looked around the room and her eyes stopped at Ramona. It wasn't clear exactly what had caught her attention.

"Mom?" Scott said again.

"I think we should have a toast," she said. "Nessa? Would you like to do the honors?"

Ramona loudly swallowed. "Sure. Yeah."

"Great," Debra said. She stood up and raised her glass in the air.

Everyone else followed.

"Hmm," Ramona said. "Well, I think we should toast to Debra for making an amazing recovery. So … cheers." She leaned forward to clink glasses.

Debra stopped her from completing the cheers. "That's not enough. I'm old news, dear. Let's hear what you're thankful for."

Scott couldn't help but think that this was a weird moment. Their family wasn't known for toasts.

"Okay," Ramona said, "Let's raise our glasses to Jeffrey, for being awesome at killing space mutants. And Rob, even though he's not here, for being a tireless businessman and an excellent … brother-in-law. And to Scott, for being my best friend and the strongest guy I know. Cheers."

Clink.

"Hear, hear!" Jeffrey said.

Debra smiled. Ramona looked pleased with herself. But Scott couldn't help thinking that the toast—no matter how positive—was a very *Ramona* thing to say.

•••

Creak!

There was one step in the McInney household that always made noise. Usually, Scott stepped over it, but that night, he had other things on his mind.

He'd just said good night to his mom and left her bedroom as quietly as possible. As he stepped off the stairs, though, he heard loud noises filling the whole.

No. Not noises. Laughter.

Rob, Jeffrey, and Ramona were in the living room, laughing hysterically.

Uh-oh.

He could tell by Rob's face that Ramona had just told him something really embarrassing. The biology class frog episode? Breaking Miss Norris's lawn gnome? Or maybe the time they tried ghost hunting? As his older brother, Rob had front-row tickets to plenty of Scott's childhood embarrassments, but there were still a few stories that he and Ramona had kept quiet.

"What did I miss?" Scott said with a sigh.

"Uncle Scott. You went ghost hunting?"

He glared at Ramona. In response, she shrugged. "It just slipped out."

"I'm sure it did."

Rob couldn't stop laughing, and even though Jeffrey didn't quite understand what was going on, he was laughing too. Rob had a box of leftover pizza in his hands. Even though he'd missed dinner, he'd still get to enjoy the extra anchovy slices.

"You do realize that we swore each other to secrecy," Scott said. "You realize that, right?"

"Things change," she said.

Yes, Scott thought, *they certainly do.*

Rob wiped his eyes and shook his head. It was time to get serious. "Can we talk?" he asked. But the underlying question was: Can we talk without Mom hearing us?

"She's asleep," Scott answered. "The coast is clear." He sounded like they were eight-year-olds playing Seize the Flag.

"Is this about … money?" Ramona asked. Scott knew that his brother would've been offended by such a personal question from someone other than Ramona.

Rob turned to his son. "Jeffrey, why don't you go play in the backyard, 'kay?"

"But Dad—"

"Go."

And he went. Like most little kids, he could tell when the adults were about to start their adult-talk.

Now Rob was free to answer Ramona's question. "It's about money."

"What happened now?" Scott asked.

For the last few months, things had been really touch and go with Rob's company. At first he said the usual catch-all excuse: "Tough economy." But then Rob started selling off property, vehicles, even things around the house. He laid off two of his employees. Just before Debra's accident, he'd told Scott—and Scott alone—that if things didn't get better for McInney Renovations, he'd lose his house.

He looked at Ramona, who was only vaguely aware of the situation. There was a whole iceberg of financial problems for Rob, and Ramona only saw the tip.

"Don't look so serious," Rob said. "It's actually good news."

"Really?"

"Really?"

"I have a potential client. A big one."

"That's great news," Scott said.

"In Chicago."

"That's … um …"

"Exactly. Jeffrey's going to stay with friends, so you don't have to worry about babysitting. But …"

"You'll be away from Mom."

"I'll be away from Mom."

Scott knew his brother wanted his blessing. Otherwise he would've just said it in a crappy text message. But Scott didn't know if he was ready to give his okay. After all, their mother needed them there. She needed family.

Not for the first time that week, Scott McInney was at a loss for words.

So Ramona chimed in. "If it's something you have to do, then it's something you have to do."

"When do you leave?" Scott asked.

"Tonight. Midnight. It was the earliest flight."

"You already booked your flight."

"Yeah."

Once again, Ramona chimed in. "Well, good luck! Remember, firm handshakes make a world of difference." Sometimes, she just said things to fill the silence.

Scott and Rob hugged and Scott said, "Get back soon." That was the best he could do.

"And I'll definitely be back before Mom's big party," Rob said. "And listen, I wouldn't go if I didn't think you had everything under control."

There really wasn't anything else to say, so they stood there silently for a while until Ramona broke the tension. "So, Scott, if you still have your ghost-hunting equipment, maybe we can check out the basement."

They didn't have a basement.

Rob noticed the way that his brother looked at Ramona. He gave Scott a warning look. *Watch out,* it seemed to say. Scott noticed this instantly.

"Sorry, Ramona. I'm afraid all that stuff is long gone. But you can always go to Walmart and stock up for us. I think their paranormal section is across from home and garden."

She smiled. "I'd better head out. See you tomorrow."

And she left.

Scott couldn't help but watch her go. When she exited a room, it was like the whole atmosphere changed, like there was suddenly something missing that would never come back. He wondered if anyone else felt that way about her.

Probably not.

She was unique. And his feelings for her—his weird, *friend/not friend* feelings—were unique too.

Rob grabbed his shoulder. For a second there, he'd forgotten that his brother was even in the same room, let alone standing a few feet away.

"Dude," Rob said.

"Don't start," Scott said.

"What? I wasn't gonna—"

"Just don't, okay?"

Rob squeezed. "What I was going to say," he said, "was that this fake-wife thing is a little weird."

"Come on."

"But!" Rob continued. He held up one finger. "But it's good to have her back."

Scott nodded.

"Just make sure things don't go too far." Rob let go.

Always the older brother. Always looking out for everybody else, even when he leaves. Some things never changed.

Chapter Nine

Debra laughed so hard, she snorted. That made Ramona laugh, too, and pretty soon, no one could stop them. They were in the midst of a potent case of giggles. After a good two minutes of fanning their faces and trying to talk, Ramona finally gained a small bit of composure.

"What are we even laughing about?" she asked.

Debra snorted again. "I don't even remember anymore."

Ramona knew it had something to do with her childhood, something really embarrassing from high school, but for the life of her, she couldn't remember. "Come on," she said. "We've been at this for an hour. We have to set out the rest of these tables before Scott comes home."

They'd been planning the party for the last three days now, and everything was moving along like a high-speed train. At this pace, they could reschedule everything for tomorrow, and they'd be in a good place—with the exception of Debra's health. Sure, she'd come a long way in three days of walking and talking, but she still wasn't at her A-game. If only her body was as cooperative as these damn decorations.

Still, Debra said she hadn't laughed like that in ages, so Ramona took it as a definite good sign.

Right now, they were positioning all the patio furniture in the backyard, spacing out the chairs and lining up the tables. The awning was already in place, so they had to make sure all the seating was out of the sun.

Ramona took a quick break by sitting on one of the tables.

Debra glanced down at Ramona's legs. "What's that?" she asked.

Ramona followed her gaze, but couldn't see anything. "What? Did I step in something again?"

"No, your knee," the older woman clarified. "That scar looks a lot like … your sister's."

Ramona gulped. Sure enough, her right knee had a small triangular scar right in its center. And out of all the physical traits that she and Nessa shared, that wasn't one of them. She had to think quickly, or else Debra would know something was up. "Oh, um, that wasn't Ramona. That was me, remember?"

Debra shook her head. "No. I clearly remember Ramona falling in the backyard. Right over there, see? By the hydrangeas? You weren't there. You were showing off your new dress to the boys across the street. And I very clearly remember giving her a Flintstones Band-Aid. She always loved Flintstones more than you."

All of that was true: the fall, the hydrangeas, the Flintstones bandage. She didn't know how to get out of this one, so she decided to dig herself in deeper. "Debra, no. That was me, remember? Ramona hated the Flintstones. She thought their big, bare feet were creepy. I was the one who fell."

Debra cocked her eyebrow. She studied Ramona for a second.

Ramona felt a knot in her stomach. It twisted and twisted.

"I guess my brain's not what it used to be," Debra finally said.

"Oh, don't say that."

She looked away sadly. "No, it's true. And I'm sorry I brought up Ramona. I know you two aren't on the best terms right now."

"Why do you say that?"

"Because she hasn't visited me yet," Debra answered matter-of-factly. "Your sister loves me, just like I love both of you. But she hasn't come over once, and I assume it's not because of something I did mid-coma. So that leaves sister problems."

Debra's assumptions were completely wrong, but they did seem like a good excuse to cover up the real issues. Ramona decided to play along. "Yes. Since the wedding, she's been a little distant."

"Say no more," Debra said. "Like I told you, I'm sorry for bringing it up."

"Oh no," Ramona answered. "It's okay. You can talk about Ramona all you want. You were like a mother to both of us, remember? And I'm sure she'll see you really soon."

Debra began straightening the last of the patio tables. They could've been finished with this thirty minutes ago, but the conversation had gotten too serious. "When I see her, I know what I'll tell her, too."

Ramona scooted all the chairs together. "And what's that?"

"I'd tell her that if a woman loves a man, she has to fight for him at all costs. But"—and she raised her voice for this last part— "if two women love the same man, they each have to respect his decision. You can't make someone love you any more than you can make the ocean stand still. If it's meant to be, it'll happen."

Ramona felt that familiar sensation: a clamp around her heart. She was getting used to that feeling. "You should really tell her that," she said.

"And I will," Debra promised. "*When* she comes to see me." Having moved all the patio chairs except one, Debra sat on the last chair and stretched her legs onto the table. "Your sister did get one thing right, though," Debra said.

Ramona leaned close. "And what's that?"

"Fred Flintstone had really creepy feet." She started laughing again.

Reluctantly, Ramona joined her.

• • •

An unexpected gust of cool air brushed across Scott's face. The surface of the Colorado River rippled and changed direction. For now, this place was paradise. Scott tried to forget all his worries and troubles; he tried to wipe his mind clean and just enjoy his surroundings.

He could certainly use a break from all the confusion.

He kept his leg submerged in the rushing waters. He slowly ate the second half of his tuna sandwich, pausing every few bites to throw a few crumbs of bread into the water. He made sure not to throw any of the tuna into the water; that would send the wrong impression to all those fish down there waiting for him to finish the last round of river habitats.

Every day, Scott ate a tuna sandwich with mustard and tomato slices, and every day, he made sure the schools of fish under his feet didn't know that he was eating their cousin.

Quinn and Terry sat on the other edge of the dock, enjoying their sandwiches and Cokes. Miguel had forgotten his lunch, so he'd offered to work through the break and leave a few minutes early at the end of the day. Scott noticed that Miguel conveniently forgot his lunch every time he had a hot date to prepare for. Whatever. As long as he pulled his weight during work hours, Scott couldn't complain.

A floating branch jabbed into Scott's submerged feet. The current was definitely wild today, especially after all the heavy rains they'd been having way upstream. He quickly pulled his legs out of the water.

Next to him, Miguel chucked one of the second to last fish habitats into the river. It landed with a splash before the pair of sandbags dragged it to the bottom. He grunted in self-satisfaction.

Scott noticed that Miguel's ratty sneakers were untied. Normally, this wouldn't be a big deal. BLM guys didn't have the strictest dress code. But their safety code was written in stone—or at least heaps of government paperwork—and a loose shoelace was a definite violation of that. If his shoelace caught on even a single branch, he could get pulled underwater before anyone would even know he was gone.

"Tie your shoes, Miguel," Scott warned.

His coworker looked at him blankly. "Sure thing, boss," he said, but he didn't actually tie anything. Odds are, Miguel hadn't read the safety handbook.

Miguel picked up the last of the fish habitats—a small cluster of plastic pipes bound together by dried Christmas tree branches—and hoisted it into the water. If he had listened to Scott's instructions, his shoelace wouldn't have gotten tangled in the branches. He didn't, though, and the weight of the habitat yanked him off his feet. He toppled into the water, his body twisting in mid-air.

If only he had listened to Scott's instructions—

If only—

Miguel was pulled underwater. If someone didn't help him, he would drown in minutes.

Scott didn't have a single thought in his head. His entire body was on autopilot. There was no fear or anxiety in him, only an electric drive, an urge that propelled him forward.

He dove into the river.

• • •

Ramona stepped out of her car, armed with silverware and a Tupperware container stuffed full of meatloaf. "Okay," she whispered to herself. "You're just dropping off Scott's lunch. No need to be nervous."

She was nervous, and she really didn't know why. She had a weird sense of foreboding about this afternoon. She was afraid that without his mother there, she'd say the wrong thing, push things too far too fast. No matter how well things had been going the last couple of days, their friendship was still on the mend.

She almost hadn't come, but this whole thing was Debra's idea. "Here. Take this to his work. He'll love you even more." She was certainly insistent.

Ramona hadn't argued, even though she knew that Scott was probably already eating his trademark tuna sandwich with mustard and tomato slices. It was never easy to argue with Debra McInney, especially now that she was in recovery. Somehow, those extra months of sleep had brought out her argumentative streak. It was like she'd spent all those nights in the hospital stockpiling her arguments, waiting for the moment when she'd wake up and unleash them upon the world.

The other reason Ramona didn't protest to this lunch delivery was that she genuinely wanted to see Scott in his workplace. She hadn't come to visit BLM land for more than a year, and she missed the endless Arizona horizon and the dark blue river. It was such a peaceful environment, so calm and relaxing and—

"Quinn! Go inside! Call an ambulance!"

A panicked scream ripped through the silence, and Ramona recognized the voice right away as Scott's younger coworker, Terry. She'd talked with him a few times in the past, but his voice had never sounded that terrified.

Right in front of her, Ramona saw a large figure dive head-first into the river. She didn't see his face, but she could tell from his wide frame and her own panicked intuition that the figure was Scott.

Scott McInney diving into dangerous waters.

Scott McInney playing the hero.

Her Scott McInney.

In the sudden rush of fear, she didn't realize that the Tupperware fell from her hands and landed on sandy ground. She didn't realize that she sprinted toward the dock like an Olympic gold medalist. She also didn't realize—and this was probably for the best—that she was screaming bloody murder.

Quinn rushed toward the water. Terry ran for help. And the river's surface didn't break.

He was down there, and he wasn't coming up.

Her first thought was: *What will Debra think?* She pictured herself walking back to McInney Manor, breaking the bad news to Debra. "I'm so sorry," she'd say. "There was an accident."

She pictured Debra's face as it crumpled in horror.

Don't jump to conclusions, Ramona told herself. *He knows what he's doing.*

Her stomach twisted around itself, wringing out all her gurgling stomach juices like a wet towel. She could barely breathe. Scratch that. She couldn't breathe. She could only stand, and pray, and wait.

He didn't break the surface.

The Colorado River swirled and rushed and churned. It moved south, just like it had for thousands of years, frothing around the edges and hiding countless branches and rocks.

She waited.

Oh God. She could feel the hope slowly deflating from her breathless body.

She waited.

He wasn't coming up. There was no other way to look at it. He'd dived into one of the deadliest sections of one of the deadliest rivers in America, and he wasn't coming up.

She waited.

Ramona felt like she was having a near-death experience, except Scott's life flashed in front of her eyes instead of her own. She saw glimpses of him as a kid, chasing after her, laughing, being a wild child. She saw a teenage Scott walk down the hallways of their high school, waving casually at her and lugging his football equipment. She saw—

She saw the surface break. She saw a shape appear out of the water. She saw Scott.

Scott walked onto the rocky bank, while Miguel limped along next to him. Water dripped down both of their breathless, heaving bodies. Miguel could barely breathe. Scott looked exhausted, but otherwise okay.

Something must've hit Miguel across the forehead—A rock, perhaps? Or a submerged tree branch?—because his forehead was gashed open and blood trickled into his eyes.

"Get the first-aid kit," Scott shouted toward his coworkers.

Quinn, the gray-haired guy with the trucker mustache, already had the first-aid box opened and ready to go. Scott eased Miguel onto the sandy ground, and Quinn dabbed the moisture away from his forehead before applying a bandage.

The younger kid—the surfer dude whose name Ramona always forgot—gave Scott a towel of his own. "You did good, man," he said.

Scott tried to answer, but he was too out of breath.

At that moment, as she watched Scott use the towel to wipe river water off his face and arms, Ramona came to a realization: *I can't live without him*. The thought was as terrifying as it was liberating. She needed Scott McInney in her life, and not just as a friend.

It wasn't just a hero fixation, either, although the way he rose out of the water like a muscle-bound Aquaman certainly didn't hurt. No, Ramona wasn't the type of girl who needed a man to dive in and save her.

When Scott dove into the water, she'd had the awful feeling that she'd never see him again. She'd pictured him trapped under the current, thrashing and thrashing and then going still. And it was that image that made her come to the realization. She'd thought she'd lose him forever, and she was terrified.

Ramona watched as Scott leaned against the nearest tree, catching his breath and regaining composure. He didn't seem aware of her presence at all.

I need Scott McInney, she decided. *I need him, before it's too late.*

And even though this was a sudden realization, it was something she'd kept inside her for months. Years, even. In fact, this was probably why she hadn't been sleeping. She was incomplete, and she finally knew why.

Now, all she had to do was act on it—just not today. Before anyone could notice her presence, she picked up the spilled meatloaf, backed into her car, and drove away. Things would have to wait.

Chapter Ten

Jeffrey reached for a dinner roll, but Scott swatted his hand away. "Wait till your grandma sits down," he whispered.

"Oh," Jeffrey said, sounding grave and adult. "Of course." He folded his hands in his lap and waited politely. Even though his dad wasn't even in the same time zone, he made sure to keep courteous and polite. Ramona watched him with amusement. At times, he acted like a typical seven-year-old—ice cream on his face, mud on his jeans—but other times he acted like a miniature businessman, just like his father.

"She'll be back in a second," Ramona assured him. "She's just scooping up the last dish."

Jeffrey nodded. "No hurry."

Ramona and Scott exchanged smiling glances. He still hadn't mentioned the near-drowning, to her or to anyone, but she assumed he'd hold off on that particular story until Debra and her heart had made a full recovery.

Scott sat next to her, close enough for her to feel his warmth. He'd just taken a shower to wash off all of the grime and dirt from his job, so he smelled fresh and clean. His hair was still a little wet.

Jeffrey sat across from them, wearing the Pokemon T-shirt he'd worn at least once a week for the last year. It was starting to unravel around the edges, and the ironed-on Pikachu looked faded and droopy, but it was his favorite.

Rob's chair was empty, of course, but Debra set a plate for him anyway. She was just like that.

Finally, after two minutes of Jeffrey desperately trying to stop himself from fidgeting, Debra walked into the dining room with the last bowl of mashed potatoes. "I hope everyone's hungry!"

she said. She looked like she'd just stepped out of a Thanksgiving greeting card, or a kitchen catalog.

Scott leaned over to Ramona and whispered, "This is her first time cooking since she woke up."

It took a few seconds for Ramona's brain to register what a big deal that was. All her adult life, Debra's identity had been tied up with her cooking skills. Every birthday, every holiday, she spent more time in the kitchen than with her guests. She loved to cook. She was proud of her skill in the kitchen. Now that she was cooking again, it meant that she was finally—*finally*—back to normal.

Debra slipped a little as she placed the bowl onto the table.

Well, Ramona thought, *she's* almost *back to normal. She's still too weak.*

Jeffrey looked at the steaming mashed potatoes with wonder in his eyes. Without thinking, he reached toward the bowl with his hands. Debra slapped them away.

"I'm sorry, Grandma," Jeffrey said.

"It's okay." Debra slid the serving spoon across the table.

Jeffrey served himself, and then—with some effort, because his arm span wasn't very long—he reached across the table and served Debra, Scott, and Ramona, too.

"Thank you, Jeffrey."

"Thank you, Jeffrey."

"Thanks, big guy."

Jeffrey smiled, showing off his latest missing tooth. "I wish Dad was here," he said, "so I could give him some potatoes, too!"

Everyone dug in. The McInney family wasn't the type to say grace before meals. They only went to church on Christmas and for funerals. Plus, Debra always said that if you wanted to thank someone for the delicious food, it might as well be her. God didn't slave over a hot stove.

After a few delicious mouthfuls, Ramona turned toward Scott and whispered, "Could you pass the salt?"

He did, and their fingers touched for the briefest of moments. They exchanged smiles.

"How was work, son?" Debra asked.

"Uneventful," Scott lied. Ramona wasn't surprised that he avoided the topic of almost dying. Perhaps he'd tell her one day— and perhaps Ramona would tell *him* that she saw him dive into the water. One day.

Debra then turned toward her fake daughter-in-law. "How's the job hunt going?" she asked.

Ramona had to think of an answer fast. While she worked full time at the library, her sister was currently unemployed. In fact, Nessa hadn't held a steady job since sophomore year of high school, when she'd worked at the hot dog place that always gave her free bottles of ketchup.

"Still looking," she admitted.

"Any interviews this week?" Debra pressed.

Ramona glanced at Scott. *What should I say?*

"She got a call-back from a perfume store at the mall," Scott said. It was a complete lie, but it seemed plausible. There were a few places at the mall that could be dubbed "perfume stores." And while Ramona couldn't breathe in places like that, it seemed like a natural fit for someone like Nessa.

"Fingers crossed!" Ramona added.

Debra seemed satisfied with the answer.

"I'm sure you blew them away," Scott said, laying it on thick and sweet.

"I sure hope so," Ramona said. "I'm really good at ... spritzing people." She was babbling again. To his credit, Scott didn't laugh at her awkwardness. Well, he might have chuckled under his breath.

"I'm sure you are, dear," Debra said.

Jeffrey chewed loudly.

"Not everyone figures out in first grade where they want to work," Ramona said. And it was true. Scott had stood up in the middle of Miss Holmes's first grade class and declared that he wanted to be a forest ranger. And while his current job traded the forest for the desert, it was basically the same position. He was lucky.

Scott smiled at Ramona. "I guess I've always known what I wanted."

Ramona flushed at his choice of words. He chose Nessa. He had made the wrong choice. And now she was going to prove to him how wrong that was.

"You certainly have," she said, and kissed him flat on the mouth.

He clearly hadn't been expecting that. Thankfully, he wasn't in the middle of chewing anything, or else that would've been pretty messy. He didn't pull away.

After a few seconds of interlocking lips, she pulled away first.

"Ah, you two," Debra said.

Jeffrey ate his potatoes and pretended not to notice. Sometimes, he could be pretty mature for his age.

"Scott always knows the right thing to say," Ramona said. She smiled at him.

"I'll be right back," Debra announced. "I think the gravy is hot enough." She quickly walked into the kitchen.

When the door swung shut, Scott turned toward Ramona. His mouth was flat—neither a smile nor a frown—but his eyes were wide open. "What are you doing?" he whispered.

Ramona ate another giant forkful of mashed potatoes. "Eating mashed potatoes," she said. "And they're delicious."

He ignored her joke. "That was … surprising," he said.

"Just playing the part," she said. "It's what you wanted, right?"

"Yeah … I, um …"

Ramona knew she'd caught him completely off guard. Well, not completely. He did kiss back.

Jeffrey looked at them in confusion. "Should I leave the room?" he asked.

"Stay right there," Scott said.

Jeffrey shrugged. He popped another Brussels sprout into his mouth. "'Kay."

Before Ramona could say anything else, Debra returned with another steaming bowl of potatoes. "Just what the doctor ordered," she announced.

"Great!" Ramona said. "Your mashed potatoes are my absolute favorite." She shoveled a helping and a half onto her plate. Its buttery scent filled her nostrils.

"That's strange," Debra said.

Uh-oh. "What is?" Ramona asked.

"Oh, nothing," Debra said. She silently scooped some more mashed potatoes onto Jeffrey's plate.

"What's wrong, Mom?" Scott asked.

"Oh, it's just … strange. Growing up, you never ate my mashed potatoes. You always said that you hated the chunks of potato skin that I left inside. Your sister Ramona was always the potato fan. She couldn't get enough of them."

Ramona could've kicked herself. Since she'd started pretending to be Nessa, she thought she had all her bases covered: sit with her legs crossed, laugh in a higher voice, never crack her knuckles. She thought she had everything under control. But she completely forgot about food. Nessa had polar-opposite eating preferences—vanilla instead of chocolate, beef instead of chicken—and Ramona should've remembered that. Now, most of her plate was covered in a food that Nessa would've dubbed "whitish garden vomit stuff."

She was caught in a lie and now had to crawl her way out of it. She looked to Scott for help, but he was still caught off-guard from the kiss. Then she looked at Jeffrey, as if a seven-year-old could swoop in to rescue her.

No, if Ramona Scapizi was going to get out of this one, she would have to think fast. Unfortunately, her mind was blank. The gears weren't spinning. They had ground to a halt. And all that was left inside her skull was a dull throb and the words "Holy crap holy crap holy crap" repeating over and over.

"Um," she said. "It's just …" She took another bite, trying to stall the conversation.

"She's learned to love them," Scott said. "I cook them sometimes—your recipe—and she always compliments me. I think it's probably because they're one of the only things that I can cook and she doesn't want to hurt my feelings. Isn't that right, babe?"

"Right," Ramona mumbled through a mouthful of potatoes. Relief washed over her. Scott McInney, saving people left and right.

"So I guess she's learned to love them," he said, glancing at Ramona as he said it. There was more to that statement than just potatoes. He was feeling her out, trying to figure out how much that kiss really meant to both of them.

"I guess she has," Debra said.

"And I don't remember Ramona liking them so much," he added. "I must've forgotten that about her."

"Yeah, I don't remember that, either," the real Ramona said.

"Well," Debra said, "as long as someone enjoys my cooking."

"I like potatoes, too!" Jeffrey shouted. And just like that, the conversation took a sharp right turn into all of the grandkid's favorite foods, which included most types of bubble gum, leftover meatloaf, and anything banana-flavored.

Ramona was in the clear.

While Jeffrey babbled on about how school lunches were disgusting unless chicken nuggets were involved, Ramona turned toward Scott. She didn't dare say "Thank you," but she mouthed out the words when no one else was looking.

He shrugged, and mouthed something back at her. She didn't understand him, so he repeated himself in a whisper, "No. Thank you."

•••

After dinner, Debra insisted on cleanup duty. Ramona and Scott both argued with her, but she was insistent: "It'll keep my mind sharp," she said.

Ramona didn't quite understand how rinsing off plates and sticking them in the dishwasher was a good mental exercise, but she didn't want to argue. Jeffrey offered to help, and grandmother and grandson began to clear the table.

"You two can have some alone time," Debra told them. "We won't be long."

Scott wrapped his arm around Ramona's shoulders and led her into the living room. When he knew they were out of sight, he pulled away. "So dinner was a little … interesting," he said.

"A little," she agreed. She knew she had made the first move.

"Listen," he said. "You're doing a great job pretending to be Nessa. I really believed you in there. For a second, I thought … well …"

"You almost died today," Ramona said. "I was so worried. And I thought if you had died, I wouldn't have been able to live with myself. I would've regretted not telling you …"

"You saw me today?"

"Yes."

"Wait. How? Why? I was at work. You weren't—"

"I was there, Scott. And I'm here now. And I kissed you. Now I'm just waiting for you to say something."

Scott walked over to the coffee table and readjusted a few of the family photos. He must not have realized that the first one he touched was from his wedding.

"I don't know how I feel," he said.

"It was a good kiss."

"It was a good kiss," he agreed. He looked down at the picture in his hands, and saw it for the first time. "I always liked that one," he said. "We both looked so happy."

"Yeah," she agreed. "It's such a shame you have a little wedding cake on your chin."

"What?" he said. He flipped it around. The picture fell from his hands and struck the edge of the coffee table.

"Okay," she admitted. "I lied about the cake."

They both reached for the fallen picture, their fingers touching it at the same time. Ramona waited for Scott to pull away first, but he didn't. Instead, he let his fingertips linger on the back of her hand.

Eventually, she pulled away. The butterflies in her stomach fluttered around, thrashing their wings and nibbling at her stomach lining. The only way they'd stop would be if he actually said something for once, instead of dodging all her questions.

"Hey," Scott offered. "You haven't seen my old room in a while, have you? Wanna see?"

Ramona could tell that Scott didn't realize the deeper implication of the question until after he'd said it. He was inviting her up to his bedroom. His bedroom. Sure, it was his childhood bedroom, the place where they'd spend hours building blanket forts—but the subtext remained. "Um, I mean … I think it's a better place to talk."

She nodded. "I'd like to see your room."

Together, they walked up the long staircase to the first door on the right. Of course, they had to pass by dozens of happy family pictures hanging from the wall. Most were from barbecues and birthdays. Ramona saw herself in a few of them, brighter and happier than she was now.

She pushed the door open and was greeted by a bedroom that was stuck in a time loop. Dark green blankets matched the duck-print wallpaper, but most of the wallpaper was covered by posters of action movies, cars, and maps. The old desk was still there, and the lamp that Ramona accidentally spilled milk on, and the bean bag chair that Nessa had accidentally torn open with her shoe. This room was a life—Scott's life—and it felt so natural to be invited back in.

"Hasn't changed much, has it?" he asked.

"Not at all." Ramona walked to the dresser and studied all the familiar knickknacks in front of her. There weren't a lot of toys; Scott had *never* collected toys as a kid. Instead, his dresser was mostly lined with things he'd found in nature: dried plants, strangely shaped rocks, ocean glass. Even as a kid, he was always interested in the outdoors.

Pushed toward the back of the dresser, hidden behind a few pencil holders, was a small treasure chest. Scott noticed it before Ramona did. "Oh," he said. "I forgot that was here."

"What is it?" Ramona asked. She ran her fingers along the uneven wood, surprised her skin didn't get jabbed with splinters. The surface felt dusty.

"It's a treasure box," Scott said. "It's mine and Nessa's." His voice was unexpectedly solemn.

Ramona examined the box closely. About a foot wide and another six inches long, it was slightly bigger than your average toaster. The whole thing was made out of cheap, unvarnished wood—cedar, perhaps?—and its edges had bronze bolts drilled into the wood. It was sloppily made and flimsy.

Scott looked up at Ramona. He tried to read her face, but apparently he didn't like what he saw.

"What is it?" she asked again.

"You don't remember, do you?" he replied.

Ramona searched her brain. Should she remember this? Did it have some sort of significance that was hidden in the back of her mind?

"No," she admitted. "I've never seen this before."

"I made this in shop class," he said. "In junior high. I got a B-minus, mostly because Mr. Phillips wanted us to varnish our projects and I ran out of time."

"I wasn't in your shop class," she said. "I didn't—"

"When I brought it home," he interrupted her, "I was so proud of it. I mean, I know it's nothing impressive, but back then I was so proud of it. I was going to give it to my parents, but they really didn't seem that interested. Rob definitely didn't seem interested. And you, well … you don't even remember it, so that tells me how impressed you were.

"But Nessa … right away, she saw it and said it was beautiful. It reminded her of the pirate ride at Disneyland. So I gave it to her and she kept it all these years. When we married, we put all our wedding stuff in here: photos, cake-toppers, her garter, everything."

Ramona wanted to reach out and open it, but something stopped her.

"It was … you know, this stupid box is one of the reasons why I knew Nessa was special. Everyone else saw it and thought it was some rough-around-the-edges piece of garbage. But she appreciated it for what it was, and it helped me realize that I loved her." He sighed for a second, reaching out to touch the box. He pulled his fingers away at the last second, as if the box would burn him. "I shoved it back there, and I haven't opened it since she left," he admitted.

Ramona put her hand on his shoulder. "She broke your heart, didn't she?"

Scott didn't answer. He didn't have to.

Ramona knew that Scott wasn't quite ready for that kiss. She would never take it back—not in a million years—but now she knew why he'd chosen Nessa, and why she'd have to wait before he chose her.

Chapter Eleven

Debra walked in on Ramona and Scott arguing about waking Debra up. Ramona thought it was a good idea, because an evening nap would really throw off her sleep schedule. Scott thought it was a bad idea, because if she was tired enough to fall asleep, then that meant that she needed sleep.

Neither of them would back down.

Fortunately, they didn't need to. Debra was awake—because of their loud arguing.

"Oh. Hi," they both said.

"Thanks for the wake-up call," Debra said. "But next time, a gentle pat on the shoulder would suffice. Do either of you want tea?"

Ramona looked at Scott, and Scott looked at Ramona. Neither had intended for things to get this heated.

"Okay, then," Debra said. "More for me."

As she puttered through the cabinets, Scott wondered if this charade was wearing down on him. He would always be glad that Ramona was back in his life, but this sort of fake romance could only go so far. Last night, she'd kissed him. For real this time. And he'd kissed her back. He'd been about to tell her he loved her, but he couldn't. He'd looked into her eyes, and Ramona didn't look back. Nessa did. That was when he knew he had to show her the treasure chest.

Because even though it was difficult for him to explain, he still loved Nessa. He was still married to her. And it would never be fair to Ramona until he made that perfectly clear.

Finally, Ramona spoke. "Debra, I think I'm going to head back to the house. *Our* house. I should probably leave you two alone for a little while." Her words were directed at Debra, but her eyes never left Scott.

"That's a wonderful idea!" Debra said. "Well, it's half wonderful. Why don't you both head out? Have you checked out the new multiplex?"

"Mom, I don't know." Scott couldn't think of any good excuse not to spend more time with his wife.

"Nonsense," Debra said. "You can both come back later. I just don't want you two cooped up here when there's so much to do."

Without any good reason why not, Scott glanced toward Ramona to see if she had anything to say.

"Sure," she said. Then Ramona took his hand, and they left together.

The happy couple.

• • •

Ramona and Scott walked through the front door at the exact same time. They were talking at the same time, too. He tried to convince her that the movie they'd just seen was awful. She tried to convince him that he was being way too hard on it, especially after she saw him jump in his seat several times throughout.

They were arguing, but it was good arguing.

Debra had waited for them to come back.

"Mom," Scott said. He'd expected her to still be up. He didn't expect her to be so—vigilant.

"Had fun?" she asked.

Ramona said, "Yes," at the exactly same time that Scott said, "No … okay, yes."

Debra smirked. That was a good sign. That meant she was feeling okay. It also meant she was still buying their act.

"I can't tell you how good it is to see you so happy together," Debra said. "You know, you're no longer officially newlyweds. The bloom should be well off the rose by now."

They exchanged glances.

"Uh, yeah," Scott said.

"And where did you two go?" his mother asked.

"We took in a movie," Ramona answered.

"Yeah, a really bad one," Scott added.

"It wasn't bad."

"Um, I could write a list."

Debra clapped her hands together. She was more than pleased that they'd had a good time. She looked somehow—proud? Scott couldn't tell.

"There were two perfectly good action movies to choose from," Scott explained. "One about cars. And one with time travel and robots."

"He loves robots," Ramona interjected.

"I've never liked robots. Anyway, I chose the genre, so she chose the movie. And we got stuck with the—"

"With the robots," Ramona finished. "And it was good. I don't think you would've liked it, Debra, but we did."

Debra said, "I hope you realize how happy I am to see you two together. I always knew you'd be a good fit."

"Really?" Scott asked.

He remembered the look on Debra's face when he'd first told her that he was dating Nessa. It wasn't a happy look.

"Well, it sounds like you had an interesting evening," Debra said. "I'll just be in the kitchen making us all some tea."

Before Debra was completely out of the room, Ramona turned to him and whispered, "We need to tell her."

"Huh?"

"You heard me."

"I did. I was just hoping that my ears were clogged from all the laser sound effects."

"We need to tell her," Ramona insisted. "I can't keep doing this. She needs to know."

Scott shook his head. "Did you see how happy she was? If she realized you weren't you, I mean …"

"Okay," she said. Just like that.

Scott knew that she understood the situation. Why was she fighting it, especially when everything was coming along so well? He worried that she was having second thoughts about the charade. He thought she might just give up.

She looked disappointed, needlessly disappointed.

"Either way," Scott said. "I had fun."

"Me too."

Scott wanted to get the last word, so he quickly added, "Robots are lame," and then left the room before she could respond.

Chapter Twelve

Ramona loved her day job. Every Monday, Wednesday, and Friday, when she wasn't taking classes or helping at McInney Manor, she was in the back room of the county library. She'd always been a bookish kid—a little too spacey, a little too imaginative—so it was no surprise that she grew up to be a librarian. Also not surprisingly, the library was like a safe haven for her.

She stood on her tiptoes and tried to reshelf a few encyclopedia volumes. At times like these, she wished she were taller than five-foot-two. (*And a half*, she always added. Five-foot-two and a half.) Even with the stool underneath her feet, it was still a struggle to reach that high.

Ramona's coworker Nancy surprised her on the other side of the shelf. She stuck her face between two copies of the *Sonoran Desert Survival Guide*. "Earth to Ramona," she whispered.

Ramona jumped back in shock. The encyclopedias flew out of her hands and slammed onto the carpet. Ramona steadied herself at the last minute; otherwise, she'd have joined the encyclopedias in a pile on the floor. "You scared me," she said.

"I've been calling your name for the last two minutes," Nancy said. "Well, whispering your name."

"That explains it," Ramona said. "I thought I was being haunted again." She laughed at her own joke.

Nancy didn't. "There's someone here to see you," she said. "It's a boy." Even though Nancy was just a few months older than Ramona, she tended to treat her like a much younger sister. Usually that meant making fun of her outfits. Sometimes—like right now—it meant treating her like a little girl about to go on her first date.

"And what boy is it, exactly?" Ramona asked. She wanted to sound coy.

"Something McInney," Nancy said. "I assume he's the boy you've been missing all your work for. He's waiting out front." Then she spun around and disappeared behind a rack of periodicals.

Ramona didn't want her heart to race every time she heard the name McInney. She didn't want to feel like the little schoolgirl that Nancy pretended she was. Ramona was an adult now, pushing twenty-eight; she was beyond the age for stomach butterflies and schoolyard romance.

Yet—

Something McInney.

Her heart raced. Her stomach fluttered. And she walked toward the front entrance, toward the "husband" who was just a friend. At first, she saw his tall outline through the frosted glass of the front windows. He bounced from one foot to the other in a decidedly non-Scott manner. She could also see through the frosted glass that he wasn't wearing his typical BLM work clothes. Did he have a—suit and tie? That didn't seem right, unless he'd stopped by on the way to a funeral or a lounge singer gig.

Ramona opened the door and met Rob.

"Hey," he said. He adjusted his tie.

"What are you doing here? Why aren't you in Chicago?" she asked. She probably should've said hello first. She was just so taken aback by his surprise visit.

"I just got back," he said, as if that answered everything. He didn't say anything about his business meetings. Had he landed the deal? Saved his business? He didn't say.

Rob was taller than his brother. Skinnier, too. Normally he looked good in his suits, but today he looked a little crumpled.

"Well, thanks for visiting," she said. "May I interest you in the latest Stephen King paperback?"

"I wanted to talk to you about Scott," he said. No smile. All business, all the time.

"Is he okay?" she asked.

"He thinks he is," Rob answered cryptically.

Ramona leaned against the nearby newspaper rack. She wanted to brace herself for some more bad news. No matter what terrible things happened to her, there was always room for more. "What do you mean?" she asked.

"This is a little difficult to say," he said, "but Jeffrey told me you and Scott had a lot of fun at dinner last night."

"Yes?"

"He said you two were really flirty."

"He did not!" Ramona protested. "He's seven. He doesn't even know that word."

"He must've learned it off *Spongebob*," Rob deadpanned, no humor in his voice. "I just wanted to make sure you understood how dangerous that could be."

"Flirtation?"

"Yes, especially with Scott."

Ramona didn't know what to say. She didn't want to tell Rob that she had feelings for his brother, and she *really* didn't want to say that he'd turned her down. But at the same time, it wasn't any of his business. How dare he act like some parental figure! He was barely two years older than she and Scott. He wasn't some wise relationship guru.

Still, she didn't feel right lashing out at him. He'd been through a lot, and it sounded like he was only looking out for his brother. So she said, "It was all an act. You know, for Debra. We were pretending to be newlyweds."

For a second, she thought he was satisfied with that answer. Then he said, "It's not an act." He smiled, but there was no warmth in it. "You're not that good an actress."

"You should've seen me as the Cowardly Lion in third grade," Ramona joked. "Grown men wept!" She had hoped her comment would somehow lighten the mood, but Rob wasn't cooperating.

They stood directly next to the newspaper racks, which meant they were both surrounded by the headlines of the day: flash floods in Colorado, an armed robbery at a Phoenix grocery store, a political coup in central Africa. So many things were happening throughout the world, and they were so much more important than Ramona's little drama. But to her, this charade was quickly becoming her life. She knew it wasn't healthy, but she couldn't control herself.

"What do you want me to do?" she asked.

He looked her straight in the eyes. "For the sake of my mother," he said, "I want you to stay away from our family."

"I'm doing this for Debra," Ramona argued, "not in spite of her. Do you really think I'd put myself through all th—"

"Yes," he cut her off.

"Well, I wouldn't," she said. "And I certainly wouldn't jeopardize your mother's health just so I could play dress-up for a week. You were there at the hospital. You know the decision Scott and I made. Why didn't you speak up then?"

"I'm sorry," he said. "I worry. About Mom. About Scott."

"Trust me," Ramona said. "Scott made perfectly clear that—"

"Listen, I know what it's like to lose a wife. It's the worst feeling in the world. It's crushing. And it's embarrassing. Everyone feels sorry for you. And you think about all the stuff you could've done differently. I can't imagine what he's going through, pretending to be married, constantly seeing a woman who looks like his wife but isn't quite real."

"I'm real," she said.

"You know what I mean." His whole tone was so unlike the Rob that Ramona had grown up with. He was always the big brother, always taking care of everybody, but he never seemed this forceful. There had to be a reason for the attitude.

"Listen," she said, "I think you're just lashing out because your business thing didn't pan out. And I'm sorry for that. But—"

"I got the deal," he said.

"What?"

"This has nothing to do with Chicago. I got the deal. Things are starting to look better for my family."

"Then why are you—?"

"Because I think you two are crossing some line," he explained. "And maybe because I'm no longer distracted by business stuff, I can finally look around me and see how messed up this fake marriage is."

He waited for her to say something, but she didn't.

"I'm sorry," he said. "I know you're in an awkward position, but please stay away from my brother." He turned around and walked away. He didn't say goodbye.

Ramona was left standing in front of the library, feeling her breath catch in her throat. Bad news in the papers surrounded her. The world was an ugly place; Ramona knew that now.

It was an ugly, ugly place.

•••

Scott pulled into the library parking lot three minutes after Ramona's shift ended at five. He barely had time to park his old Ford before he saw Ramona make a beeline across the parking lot.

She still drove that old sky-blue station wagon that her grandmother had given her. It shook too much, and the upholstery was crumbling into nothing, but she'd always loved that car. Scott was glad to see that some things never changed.

"Hey!" he shouted at her.

At first, she pretended not to hear him. Then she slowly turned around and waved.

Scott ran over to reach her.

The first thing he noticed—aside from her impatient stance—was that she was actually wearing her glasses. Ramona never wore those glasses, not out of vanity, but because she always forgot them. But they looked good on her; they really did. The thick black frames perfectly circled her eyes. They certainly made her look more like a librarian.

The second thing he noticed was that her tan skin had a natural glow in the sunlight. Why hadn't he noticed that before? Unlike Nessa, who always wore a little too much makeup, Ramona kept her skin natural, and it showed. That was one thing she didn't change for Debra's benefit.

Before he knew it, Scott had spent a whole minute noticing all the little things about Ramona—the way she always stood straight and proud, the honey glow in her hair, the single freckle next to her eye. He noticed these things because they were beautiful, and they were what differentiated her from Nessa. He should've noticed all these things before. He wasn't sure why he did now.

"Hey," he said.

"Hello, Scott." Was it just his imagination, or did she sound cold? Normally, he enjoyed listening to her voice. She had a musical quality, so even when she was talking about mundane things like parking tickets or shampoo brands, it sounded like she was happy. As a kid, he'd always thought she sounded like a Disney princess, only contemporary and slightly less innocent.

Now, though, he didn't hear any music at all. Now she sounded like a professional phone book reader.

Then again, maybe it was his imagination. He'd just caught her after a long day of school and work. Maybe she was just tired. After all, the Little Mermaid didn't have to spend nine hours a day re-shelving books based on the Dewey Decimal System.

"Is everything okay?" he asked.

"Fine," she said. A single word. Now Scott knew it wasn't his imagination. She was upset, cold. Something had gotten to her. Compared to their back-and-forth sparring at last night's dinner, she sounded practically undead.

He knew he needed to find out what was bugging her sooner or later, but he couldn't just ask her outright. Ramona wasn't the kind of girl to bare her soul that way. He needed to broach the subject in a subtle way, secret agent-style. She'd tell him. He knew she would.

"Um," he said, "I was wondering … Our fish habitat project is just about finished. I thought you'd be interested in coming down to check it out. I mean, you always said what a fascinating project it was."

"Very fascinating," she said.

"So, how about tomorrow?" he asked. "You wanna—?"

"Listen, Scott. I appreciate the offer and everything. But unless your mother is magically going to be on BLM property, I don't see the need in my presence there."

"This isn't about Mom," he said. "I thought you'd be interested. The guys and I have spent the last month and a half on these things, and I wanted to invite you, the real you."

"There is no real me," she said. Scott didn't know what she meant by that.

"So you're not interested?"

"No. Sorry." She fumbled with her car keys, but they wouldn't fit into the door. She was too distracted. "Now if you'll excuse me," she added, "I really need to get home. I haven't made a dinner for myself in days, and I was hoping to have some alone time."

"You hate alone time," Scott said.

Ramona's car keys fell out of her hands and clattered onto the asphalt. She swore loudly.

Scott crouched down to pick them up, but Ramona grabbed them before he could.

"I really appreciate the invite, though," she added.

Scott leaned against her station wagon, because he knew she hated that. He left a big handprint in the dust. "What's with the mood swing?" he asked.

"This isn't a mood swing," she said.

"I always thought your sister was the one with the mood swings," he said. Again, he wanted to strike a nerve.

"This isn't a mood swing," she said. "And maybe I'm turning into my sister. After all this pretending, she might be rubbing off on me." She retried unlocking the car door. This time, there was a click. She yanked the door open.

"That's not true," he said.

"It could be," Ramona said. "You'd better watch out, or I might run away from you, too." With that, she hopped into her car, slammed the door, and turned on the ignition. In seconds, she was down the road and out of sight.

If Scott didn't know better, he'd think that Ramona was purposely trying to push him away. She was intentionally being hurtful. He didn't know why, but he certainly knew one thing: it worked.

Chapter Thirteen

"She was just cold, guys. I don't even know."

It was a surprisingly cool day at BLM. Scott and his crew ate their lunch on the roof of the office building. Scott did most of the talking, so he still hadn't touched his tuna sandwich.

Miguel and Quinn sat cross-legged across from him, while Terry leaned over the edge and stared into the rushing river far below.

"Women," Miguel mumbled. "Like *mi abuela* always says—"

"Please stop misquoting your grandmother," Quinn cut him off. "I have some real advice for our little Romeo."

Miguel shoved Quinn, and Quinn shoved him back.

"No offense," Scott said, "but I don't know if I want to take relationship advice from either of you."

"But *mi abuela*—"

"*Or* your grandmother," Scott said.

"Then why have we been listening to your problems for the last half hour?" Miguel asked.

"Because I saved your life this week," he snapped.

Terry took the opportunity to rejoin the conversation. "Burn!" he shouted. "Damn, Miguel. You got schooled."

"Anyway," Scott continued, "I didn't tell you the rest of it. See, she kissed me."

"You mean, like, for real?" Terry asked. "Not an act?"

"Yeah," he explained. "We were at the dinner table. And it was her way of letting me know how she really feels. It was good, too."

"She took the initiative?" Quinn asked. "That seems like something Nessa would do, not Ramona."

"Wow," Miguel said. "But you're still married to her sister, right?"

"Legally, yeah," he said. "Wherever she is. And I'm just not ready to—"

"You told her that?" Quinn asked. "You told her you weren't ready?"

"Yes."

"Well, then, there you go. That's why she's cold. She put herself out there and you shot her down."

"It wasn't like that."

"It sorta was, dude," Terry said.

"But right after that," Scott said, "we had a great time together. As friends. There has to be something else that happened."

"Naw, man. I think it's just you," Quinn said, trying to sound like the voice of reason amidst all this macho, twentysomething banter. "Whatever happens, happens. The important thing is that we're all invited to your big party this weekend, yeah?"

"Yeah?"

"Yeah?"

Scott left them hanging for a second, before answering, "Of course. As long as you are on your best behavior. Oh, and Miguel …"

"What's up, boss?"

"We have a working fountain, so you better not get too close."

…

Ramona sat in the McInney back yard, struggling to connect wires and cords for the party's speaker system. She wasn't the most techno-savvy twentysomething, so it involved a lot of plugging and unplugging randomly. She might as well be defusing a bomb. With a big smile on her face, Debra sat next to Ramona and handed her a crinkled sheet of paper.

"What's this?" Ramona asked.

"Just look!"

Ramona gave up on the speaker system. Once Rob got home, he could figure it out. Instead, she unfolded the paper. There in her hands was a list of about sixty names written in scratchy blue pen. Debra's handwriting. After each name, Debra had drawn a happy face.

"Who are these people?" she asked.

Debra tried to look modest, but it wasn't working. "Oh, those are all the people I invited to our party tomorrow."

"*All* these people?"

She nodded. "And guess how many said yes."

Ramona shrugged. "Forty-two."

"All of them!" Debra shouted.

"That's fantastic!"

"I know!"

Ramona ran through the list of invitees. She recognized most of the names. "Who's that?" she asked, pointing to someone named Shirley.

"Bridge club," she answered.

"And that?"

"Bridge club."

"And that?"

"Comic book convention."

"What?"

"Bridge club."

Already, Ramona was impressed by the turnout. "And all these people said yes?" she asked.

"Every single one," Debra said.

"Wow. You're one popular lady."

"Pity points," she joked. "A coma does wonders for your social life. You should try it sometime." It was good to hear her joke about such a serious topic. Debra McInney was definitely getting her old personality back.

Ramona studied the list one more time. There was something not quite right about it. Then, it hit her. "Debra? Aren't you going to invite Ramona?"

"Your sister?" she asked.

"That's the one."

Debra blushed. Ramona had never seen her blush before. It made her seem so much younger than she actually was. "Well," she admitted, "I figured she'd visit me when she was finally ready to. You know how much I care for your sister."

Ramona nodded.

"It breaks my heart that I haven't seen her since, well, the wedding. But you know how things go."

"What do you mean?"

"Ramona was always more fragile than you," she explained. "Losing sleep over the littlest things. Once she gets over all her heartbreak, she'll come to see me. There's no sense rushing things. I figured if she wants to come forward and talk to me—about anything—she can. I'll be waiting."

Those words pierced Ramona straight in the heart. How could Debra think so little of her?

That's it, Ramona decided. *I have to come clean.*

This charade had gone on long enough. It had been more than a week already, and Debra seemed healthy enough to take the news. If Ramona waited any longer, she'd go crazy. Besides, Debra would already feel betrayed by this deception. The longer she waited, the more their relationship would be permanently damaged.

"Debra?" she said.

Debra looked up from their papers. She smiled expectantly. It was the same smile she'd always had, a special smile that only a parent would have for her child. Ramona loved her so much.

"Is something wrong?" she asked. Her voice was strong and confident. "You know you can talk to me."

Yup. This was the perfect time.

"Debra, I have to tell you something."

The older woman was clearly caught off guard by Ramona's serious tone. She accidentally dropped her papers onto the ground. "One second," she said. And as she bent over to pick them up, her whole body went slightly limp.

Panicked, Ramona reached out and steadied her. She felt like a sack of potatoes, like dead weight. Slowly, Ramona tipped her upright.

"Whoa," Debra said. "Sorry. I must've moved too quickly. Just a rush of blood to the head."

Ramona wouldn't let go. "You're okay?"

Debra pushed her away. As always, she was a proud woman. She didn't want anyone propping her up, even if she needed the support. "I'm fine. I'm fine."

Ramona looked her up and down. Sure, she looked strong and feisty. Her coloring was good and her movements were confident. But Ramona knew there was still something broken in her. Like Dr. Nguyen said, her heart needed to heal itself.

It would take time.

"So what did you want to tell me?" Debra said.

Ramona looked at Debra's wrinkled hands. They trembled slightly. Most people wouldn't even notice the movement, but Ramona did.

"Hmm?" Debra pressed.

"Oh, uh, I wanted to ask for your help with the audio equipment," she said. "I have no idea what I'm doing."

Chapter Fourteen

Rob looked like a skinner, taller version of Scott. Between the two of them, Scott got the muscles and the roguish good looks, while Rob got the book-smarts and the nine-to-five aspirations. Rob was a buttoned-up, slightly stern version of his younger brother.

At no time was this more obvious than when they were yelling at each other.

"I don't care how this whole thing started!" Rob said. "It's not healthy!"

"Not healthy?" Scott said.

"For anybody! Especially Mom! She doesn't deserve the two of you playing dress-up in front of her! And it's not healthy for you, either! And Jeffrey is all confused. Don't you think—"

"Keep your voice down," Scott scolded. "Mom's upstairs."

Because it was the night before her big party, Debra had decided to get an early night's rest. That meant Ramona was outside doing last-minute preparations, and the two McInney boys were in the kitchen making sure the food was good to go. Or at least, that was the plan. A few minutes of fridge patrol had quickly devolved into a mini-Civil War, with two brothers shouting at each other like long-lost enemies.

"I know where Mom is!" Rob said. "I'm her son, too."

"Could've fooled me," Scott answered. "Got any more business trips planned?"

They both stood in the dark kitchen. Neither had bothered to turn on the overhead light.

"That was a onetime thing!" Rob said. "I came back for her party, didn't I?"

"Look, Rob. We'll tell Mom everything. I promise. But we should do it after the party. Let's give her that, okay?"

"But what if one of the guests blabs to her?" Rob asked. "A lot of people know about Nessa. How do you think she'll take the news if she hears it on the dance floor from one of her bridge club friends?"

"I told everyone to be discreet. They all know—"

"Someone's going to slip up, Scott. You might as well come clean now."

The light clicked on overhead.

"Excuse me." Ramona walked in between them.

"Ramona!" Scott jumped.

"I was out on the porch," she explained. "I overheard things getting a little … heated."

The brothers glared at each other in strikingly similar expressions. "Not really," they said in unison.

"Great," Ramona said, looking directly at Rob. "Then you won't mind if Scott and I go outside to check out the tent situation."

Rob grumbled something unintelligible.

"What was that?" Ramona asked.

"Maybe later," Rob said, a little more confident now. "In fact, why don't you head home? We've got everything under control."

This was clearly not the answer she wanted to hear, so she turned to face Scott. He gulped. Ramona Scapizi meant business.

"Uh, Rob," Scott said, "Ramona has been really hands-on with this whole event. I think it would probably be better if she and I—"

"I don't think that's a good idea," Rob said.

"I'm not going to give in," she said matter-of-factly.

Rob shrugged. "Me neither."

"I guess I know what this means," she said.

"I guess I do, too."

Staring contest.

Rob and Ramona competed in a minute-long staring match. For a while, Scott thought that his brother would surely win this round, but Ramona wouldn't budge. She was a good head and a half shorter than Rob, so she stretched out her spine and stood on her tiptoes.

Neither blinked.

It was almost comical. The two of them had done these epic stare-downs back in elementary school, but this time seemed a little more life-or-death. Unlike before, bags of gummy bears weren't involved.

Rob looked away first. "I can't be mad at you," he said.

"Pushover," she muttered.

Rob touched her shoulder, and his smile faded into something more serious. "Watch out, okay?" he said. "Both of you. I'm not kidding about this. It's not just about Mom. It's about … this family."

Scott knew his brother meant well.

"We'll be good," Ramona said.

"Thanks," Scott added, and gave his brother a bear hug. "Why don't you take Jeffrey to the party store? We need some balloons for tomorrow."

Rob nodded solemnly. Before things could get even mushier, Scott took Ramona for a walk through the yard. The tents and dance floor were half built. Empty metal poles stuck out at weird angles. All the chairs sat in a flattened pile next to the porch.

"My brother warned you to stay away from me, didn't he?" Scott asked.

"Something like that," Ramona said.

"He's always doing that."

"Don't get mad," she said. "He's just looking out for you. For both of us. In a way, I think he might be right."

Her words hung in the air. He didn't know how to refute them, so he let them hang.

Ramona grabbed one of the tent poles and swung around it in a circle, *Singing in the Rain* style. If it didn't look so flimsy, Scott would've joined her.

"Either way, I'm glad you stared him down," he said.

"You know me," she said. "I don't blink."

The stereo system was already set up and plugged in. Scott had left it here a few hours ago, safe in the knowledge that this was spring in Farber City, so it probably wasn't going to rain any time soon.

The stereo was all set for tomorrow's party, but Scott hadn't realized he'd be using it tonight, too. He casually walked toward the speakers and pressed the power button. Instantly, a blast of static gave way to a slow pop song.

"Remember this one?" he asked, referring to the ballad.

She listened for a second before her eyes flashed recognition. "I haven't heard this since senior year."

"It's an oldie but goodie," he said. He thought this would be the perfect time to test out the dance floor—for strictly scientific purposes, of course. One must be sure the floor could withstand the weight of two dancing adults. He reached out his hand toward her.

She reached hers toward him. Instead of dancing, though, she spun her body into his arms, pulling herself as close to him as possible. Then he dipped her.

They spun around the dance floor for the rest of the song. Scott didn't know the last time he'd lost himself in a song like that. When the music finished, her fingers slipped away from his. "Wow," he said.

"Wow yourself."

"You know, you're very … graceful. I like the new you."

And he did. He hadn't been able to place his finger on it until now. Ramona was the same girl she'd always been, but now she went after what she wanted. She had grown up in her own skin. He liked that. And even though they were destined to be no more than friends, he was glad that she was here for him. He was glad that they'd danced.

"Thanks," she whispered.

"Ramona," he said. He reached forward and pulled her toward him. The next song had already started.

"I've gotta … I've gotta go," she said. She spun around to leave, but he roped his arms around her waist.

"Not so fast," he said.

She didn't bother squirming away.

"Am I crossing a line?" he asked.

"No."

"You sure? I mean, we're just having fun. I don't want you to think …"

She looked away.

"Talk to me," he said.

"You like the new me," she said.

He nodded.

"You didn't like the old me, but you like the woman that I've become, is that right?"

He could tell from her tone that whatever answer he chose, it would be the incorrect one. "I've always liked you," he said. "You know that. You're my best friend."

"You like the me who's playing a part," she said. "Because I'm not me. I'm my sister. After this week, I'll go back to being the same ungraceful, unsophisticated Ramona whom you always take for granted."

"That's not true."

She pushed herself away from him. It was like she needed room to breathe. Or fume. "You said so yourself," she said. "You like the new me. I can't keep pretending to be her for your enjoyment."

"Maybe you're right," he said. "I never meant to be unfair to you, but I think this whole situation is unfair." Before she could say anything else, he added, "Tomorrow's the big party. You'll be there, right?"

"With bells on," she said darkly.

"I'll see you there," Scott said. That was all he could ask for.

• • •

Like most nights, Ramona stared at the blinking clock next to her bed. One fifteen. All things considered, this wasn't particularly late in Ramona-time. Based on her wacked-out sleep cycle, it was practically daylight.

She had a glass of water right next to the clock. It was sweating. Below that glass, under a slowly expanding water ring, was her borrowed copy of *Anna Karenina*. She still hadn't gotten past page twelve. Normally, she'd speed through the novel like a crazy person, if for no other reason than to see how badly things end up for the title character.

But her heart wasn't in it anymore. Life was too crazy to focus on studying, or reading, or thinking at all. Well, life was too crazy for her to think about anything other than Scott McInney.

A few hours ago, they had danced together. And everything felt so right, until she realized that she wasn't even there. Nessa was.

She made a resolution to stop thinking about Scott. Whenever his handsome, rugged image came into her mind, she would push it out. Tonight, she would fall asleep on her own terms.

One twenty.

She struggled to keep her mind blank, but every few seconds it wandered back to the McInney front door. *Great,* she thought. *Another sleepless night.*

One forty.

Ramona focused on the darkness inside her eyelids. If she opened them—even a little—she'd see moon glow invade her bedroom, car headlights roll across her wall. Darkness. Blackness. It was as simple as that.

Don't think about Scott, she told herself.

Don't think about Scott.

One forty-one. She drifted off to sleep. In her dreams, she saw Scott. And he saw her, the real her. They were in the McInney backyard. All the party decorations were already up, but no one was there. Red balloons floated in the air, but otherwise everything was still.

She followed Scott through the chairs, across the dance floor, and straight toward the old treehouse. He pointed up.

"You want me to go up there?" she asked.

He didn't answer. Instead, he started climbing.

Dream logic was a funny thing. In dreams, you could do the most nonsensical things, but it made complete sense in the moment. Right now, though, Ramona felt strange climbing up to the treehouse. She hadn't been inside in years. It was a symbol of her childhood, nothing more. It wasn't a place she was meant to revisit.

Scott disappeared through the trap door.

Ramona had no other choice but to follow. She climbed up the tree, which seemed to stretch on and on, way up into the sky. She pushed the door open, and crawled inside.

"I thought you'd never come," Scott said. And he closed the door behind her.

For the rest of the night, Ramona had a huge smile on her face. It was the best night's sleep she'd had in years.

Chapter Fifteen

A single red balloon bobbed over Scott's head. There were dozens more where that came from, but he focused all his attention on that one red balloon.

Not because it was a particularly special balloon.

Not because he was interested in where it would end up.

He stared at that one red balloon so that no one would notice him gawking at Ramona Scapizi when she made her grand entrance.

He still gawked, though. He couldn't help it. Besides, it didn't matter what anyone thought. Right now, she was his wife.

Ramona stepped through the crowd, wearing white, oozing confidence. Scott had no clue why all the other men at the party didn't instantly drop their champagne glasses and gawk too. She was stunning. And she walked directly toward Scott.

As she passed that stupid red balloon, she poked it with her finger. It somersaulted through the air.

"Looking good," he said.

"Back at you, Scott Boy," she said. "I don't know if I've ever seen you in a tie before."

"Sure you have," he said. "Elementary school. My catechism. You were there. Oh, and I wore a tie to graduation. And the wedding … I … " He instantly wished he could take back that last part, the part about the wedding. He knew how much Ramona hated that word.

But this time, she didn't react at all. She smiled and readjusted his tie. "Listen," she said, "I'm sorry I was weird last night. I figured if I'm going to be your wife for one more day, I might as well make the most of it."

"Great," Scott said. "Once this party's over, things can finally get back to normal."

"That's all I ask," she said. "After all this lying, I'm starting to get worried about my eternal soul. Is it too late for me to go to catechism, too?"

"I think you have to be Catholic for that," Scott said.

They looked at each other for the longest time, neither knowing what to say. It was comfortable silence, but it was clear they both had a sense that there was something important, something left unsaid.

"I'm a little sad to see this end," Ramona admitted. "But at the same time, thank God."

Scott shrugged, but deep down, he agreed. On both counts.

"You ready to do this?" she asked. "One more time? As man and wife?"

He hooked his arm around hers, and together, they walked out into the crowd. And even though Ramona was still posing as her sister, Scott didn't feel like he was hiding anything. Not anymore.

• • •

Debra stood at the center of the party and raised her champagne glass into the air. "Attention, everybody. Attention. It's toast time!"

Rob switched off the music. The rest of the guests took the hint and quieted down.

Debra looked stunning in an emerald green dress and all her favorite jewelry. Her long honey-gray hair cascaded down her neck in waves; only Ramona and Dave the barber knew that extensions were involved. She leaned against a nearby table—not for support, Ramona knew, but just to look good.

"Will everyone please raise their glasses?"

Ramona looked all around her for the champagne glass she'd just set down. When she couldn't find it anywhere, she grabbed a (hopefully) unclaimed glass from the nearest table.

"I think I'm supposed to stand next to her," Scott whispered. Before Ramona could object, he ran off to stand next to his toasting mom.

"As you all know," she said, "I've been sleeping for a long time now. A very long time. I finally woke up this month, thanks to the tireless doctors at Farber Memorial. I'm still not 100 percent yet, but I'm damn close. And I invited everybody here to say 'Good morning,' and to show off how amazing I look."

The crowd chuckled.

"Now, I couldn't have done this without the help of my two sons, Rob and Scott; my grandson Jeffrey; and, of course, my beautiful and talented daughter-in-law, Nessa McInney." She waved her champagne glass in Ramona's direction.

Ramona felt her face flush with heat. She'd never been good at accepting compliments. She'd much rather be insulted, because at least then she didn't have to act gracious about anything. What did they want her to do? Bow? She waved awkwardly.

"A few weeks after she joined the family," Debra continued, "I fell asleep. But now I'm finally able to spend some time with the newest McInney. Nessa, thank you so much." She raised her glass high into the air. "Everybody, cheers!"

"Cheers!"

Ramona gulped.

• • •

Confetti littered the ground. Red balloons bobbed in the air. Streamers stretched across the sky from tree to tree. So far, Debra's waking party was a huge success.

Ramona casually leaned against a tree trunk and drank her half-cold bottle of Coors Light. Terry and Miguel, the two youngest BLM workers, stood on either side and lobbed questions her way:

"So what are your intentions with Scott?"

"Are you anything like your sister?"

"You do know his heart is broken, right?"

"Do you come from a good family?"

"Are you a registered voter?"

Ramona tried her best to answer each one as earnestly as possible, but they kept throwing more and more questions her way. It was obvious they just wanted to catch her off guard. Maybe they thought if they spoke fast enough, she'd crack and say, "Okay, okay. I did murder that guy. But he had it comin'."

Terry and Miguel had seen too many *Law and Order* reruns.

"So how do you feel about Scott?" Terry asked in his typical surfer-dude voice.

Ramona didn't have to think about her answer. "I love him," she said. "And I hate him, too. Depends on the hour."

Miguel and Terry exchanged glances, as if they were jurors carefully deliberating a key piece of testimony. They came to a silent conclusion. Terry nodded.

"Well?" Ramona asked.

"That sounds like our Scott," Miguel said. "You have our blessing." Then he raised his beer, and the three clinked bottles.

"Thanks," she said, "but I'm his friend. That's it. And once this party's over, I'll go back to being his friend. It's like a Cinderella thing." That sort of put a damper on the cheers, but that didn't stop Ramona from downing her beer.

...

Scott watched Ramona hit it off with his buddies. He'd known she had the hidden superpower of hanging-out-with-the-guys, but he hadn't realized how natural she looked when faced with Terry's and Miguel's idiotic questions. He couldn't hear what they were saying, of course, but their smiles told the whole story.

He was just about to join them, when—

"Scott!"

Before he knew it, Quinn surprised Scott by wrapping his arm around Scott's shoulders.

"Hey, um … didn't see you there," Scott mumbled.

Quinn laughed, revealing a definite hint of Scotch on his breath. Scott wasn't used to his older coworker acting tipsy. They weren't in the same age bracket, after all, so they seldom hung out in their off hours. But it was kind of nice to see his coworker enjoying himself. He looked like a lumberjack on a bender.

"Look, man," Quinn said, slurring his words only slightly, "I know you didn't ask my opinion, but thumbs up, my man!" With that, he gave Scott two big thumbs-up.

"I'm glad you're enjoying yourself," he said.

"No," Quinn said. "Not the party. It's a little boring. I mean, thumbs up on Ramona. She's a good one. She's good."

"You're babbling," Scott said.

"No! I've never been more sober in my life. And I don't babble. And Ramona is a good girl. We like her. A lot. So, yeah." And with that, he turned around and walked back to the open bar.

"We're friends," Scott called out to him, but his words were ignored.

Even though Quinn was about two mojitos away from thoroughly embarrassing himself, Scott knew that he was right. Ramona was awesome. He was so happy to have her back in his life.

He glanced in her direction. She was still standing by Terry and Miguel. The three of them were laughing over something— probably some embarrassing story from Scott's past. She noticed him staring, and she waved in his direction.

He waved back.

God, she looked beautiful in her tight white dress. She'd taken her shoes off a few minutes ago, so now she was barefoot in formalwear.

He watched as she said her goodbyes to Terry and Miguel, and then she walked toward him. Classical music wafted through the air, something slow, something he'd heard before. Her hips swayed. Her hair danced lightly in the wind. She was coming for him, and his heart soared.

For the first time in a long time, Scott felt speechless. No, it was more than that. It was—breathless. There was a stunned emptiness inside him, and he wasn't quite sure what that meant. He had to will himself to breathe.

"Hey," Ramona said.

"Hey."

"I think you should ask me to dance," she said.

It took him a while to form words, both because his brain was on slow-mo and because he didn't want to sound like a cartoon character babbling "Hummina-hummina" at a pretty girl. Eventually, he forced himself to breathe, and he asked, "Would you care to dance, Miss Scapizi?"

She crinkled her nose. "I thought you'd never ask."

He gently placed his hands around her waist and led her to the middle of the dance floor. The music got louder: slow, classical, lots of violins. Together, they danced.

Moving with her, holding her, feeling her—it just felt so natural. It felt like the most natural thing in the world, like his whole life was spent waiting for the moment he could glide across a dance floor with Ramona Scapizi. He certainly wasn't a dancer—never had been—but he didn't feel awkward. His feet knew where to go. His hips knew how to move. His hands knew when to pull her close, and when to dip her back. It was different than their dance last night. Maybe it was all the people watching them. Maybe it was the realization that this would be the last night that they were "married." This was special.

They danced for three songs, but it felt like seconds. There might have been other people on the dance floor, but Scott couldn't be certain. He wasn't certain of anything anymore, except that he felt okay. All his worries about Debra, and work, and the wreckage of his failed marriage—they all went away with this song. The only thing that mattered was the music.

For a second, Scott noticed his mom sitting underneath the awning. She was watching him—watching *them*—and apparently she liked what she saw. Their eyes met, and Debra waved at her son. He nodded back at her. Despite everything she'd been through, Scott knew she was going to be okay.

Suddenly, Ramona froze mid-step. Her eyes widened.

"What's wrong?" Scott asked. "I hope I didn't step on your toes again." He meant it as a joke, but she wasn't laughing. It was like she didn't hear him at all.

She stared just over his shoulder. There was something in the distance. Based on her expression, Scott couldn't tell if it was a good something or a bad something, but he knew it was important.

"What is it?" Scott asked again. He should've turned around for himself, but he was afraid of what he'd see. Besides, he didn't want to pull away from Ramona, not even for a second.

Ramona heard him this time. In response, she pointed toward the distance. Her hand was shaking.

Slowly, Scott turned around to see for himself. There, at the edge of the yard, was a beautiful woman in a red skirt.

A beautiful woman who looked exactly like the woman in his arms.

"Nessa," Scott whispered, as if he was seeing a ghost. After all, maybe he was.

Chapter Sixteen

Scott couldn't believe it. Nessa Scapizi—the uninvited guest from his past, the wife who ran away—was at his party. More importantly, Nessa Scapizi was walking right toward him.

Ramona's hands dropped away from his shoulders.

"Give me a second," Scott said. He walked toward his wife, leaving Ramona, Debra, and an entire party behind.

Nessa looked exactly the same as the last time he saw her. Her outfit was different, red now instead of eggshell white, but everything else was the same. Well, her expression was different, too. Her expression was dead serious.

When she reached Scott, he didn't know what to do. Should they shake hands? Should he hug her?

Somehow sensing the confusion, Nessa made the first move: She hugged him. His heart shuddered. *She* hugged *him*. She initiated the contact; she chose him. But he quickly realized that the hug was perfunctory, cold. The curve of her body didn't mesh well with his, and when she finally pulled away, it wasn't nearly fast enough.

"Nessa," he said. "What are you—?"

"I heard about your mom," she said. "I've been dreading coming back, but I figured now would be the best time."

She was wrong, of course. Dead wrong. *Now* was the absolute worst time for her to make a surprise appearance.

He noticed the worn manila envelope in her hands. "Divorce papers?" he asked.

"Divorce papers," she said. "I'm sorry. I was just going to slip them into the house, but I saw you there and I just ..."

Scott rolled up the envelope and shoved it in his back pocket. He didn't bother opening it. He trusted her. More importantly, he didn't want to set eyes on the damn things. He pictured pages and pages of legalese in tiny fonts. He pictured a blank line where he had to sign his name, sitting right next to Nessa's signature that was already there. He knew the drill. He'd seen movies.

He felt eyes on the back of his neck. People were watching him. A whole party's worth. Silently, he grabbed her shoulder and guided her behind the edge of the porch. When he was sure no one was watching or listening, he asked, "Where were you? This whole time … I …"

"What?" Nessa asked. Her eyebrows creased. "You didn't know?" She looked genuinely surprised by his question, and that only made him angrier.

"Of course I didn't know!" he shouted. "You left in the middle of the night. You didn't tell anyone. You didn't even tell your sister!"

"I didn't," she said, her eyes quickly glancing toward Ramona. "But I told you."

"What are you talking about?"

Nessa reached out and held Scott's hands. This time, the contact felt genuine. It didn't feel like love, per se, but it was definitely caring, compassion. "I left you a note," she said. "In our treasure chest. I knew you'd look inside, because it was such a special object for both of us."

Oh God. The treasure chest that he refused to open. The treasure chest with so many bad memories.

"You really didn't know?" she asked.

He shook his head. "I never read the note."

She didn't apologize. Instead, she whispered, "Look at me." Scott didn't realize he wasn't giving her eye contact.

He did. He saw that her eyes were slowly filling up with water. One part of his heart wanted to hold her, and the other part wanted to slap himself across the face for feeling such things.

"I see you," he said.

She laughed. He didn't know why. "I lied to myself," she said. "For weeks, for months, I told myself that I was the right girl for you. I told myself that you picked me."

"I did pick you," he said.

"No, you didn't," she corrected. "You thought you did, but you were lying to yourself. I didn't know for sure until the first few nights we spent together as a married couple. You talk in your sleep. You know that, right? You whisper words in your sleep. And every night, you whispered her name."

"Who?" But he knew the answer: Ramona.

"You married me because I was the next best thing. But your heart was never fooled. You love Ramona, and you always have."

"It's a different kind of love," he said.

"No, it's not. It's the only kind. It started out as friendship, but you know very well that it grew into something more. You were too afraid to act on those feelings, because you didn't want to lose her, so you chose me instead. Have your cake and eat it too."

"I ..."

"I left," Nessa continued, "because I wanted you to sort things out with her. And because I was too embarrassed to watch it happen. All that was in my note ... which you didn't read, because you're a big, dumb idiot." She shoved him a little, but it was more playful than angry.

Well, mostly playful.

"I'm sorry, okay?" he said.

"Me too." Once again, her eyes danced with moisture.

"Why didn't you come before?" he asked.

"I tried to visit a few times," she said. "I drove by the house and everything. But each time, it felt wrong. When I heard about your mom waking up, I knew this was it. Now or never. Is she okay? I'd really like to see her."

"That's probably not the best idea," he said.

"I understand," she said. "And I'm glad you're moving on."

"Why do you say that?"

"I saw you dancing with Ramona," she said. "You two were happy, just like I figured you'd be."

"Ramona and I aren't together," he said.

The tears had dried from her eyes. In their place was a look of pure anger. "How dare you?" she said.

"It's not like that. We kissed, but I was still …"

"I loved you," she said. "You do know that. But deep down, I knew that you loved her. When I couldn't delude myself anymore, I left. It was the noble thing to do."

"There's nothing noble about running away," he said.

"It was the hardest thing I ever did, okay? But I knew you and my sister would be happier together. It was noble," she said. "It was noble."

"But I don't …"

At that moment, Ramona stepped out of the trees. Scott could tell she'd just come from the bathroom. Her face glistened a little with sink water.

"Ramona," her sister said. She ran to hug her sister, but Ramona pushed her away.

"Stop trying to force us together," Ramona said. "He doesn't feel that way. How many times does he have to tell you?"

"Scott," Nessa said. "I think you should leave. My sister and I need to talk."

Scott looked at them both, so similar in so many ways. He loved one of them, and it was tearing him apart trying to figure out whom.

• • •

Nessa and Ramona stared at each other for the longest time. Then, like a rush of water, then ran to each other and embraced.

Tears flowed from Ramona's eyes. She knew how good it felt to hold her sister again. No matter what wreckage was left in her wake, at least she had her sister back. At least she knew Nessa was okay.

"I'm so sorry," Nessa said.

"I'm sorry, too," Ramona replied.

Quickly, Nessa pulled away. "Don't say that. You have nothing to be sorry about. I should've … I should've called you. I should've …"

"Yeah," Ramona said. "You should've." She pulled away. And just like that, she regretted ever apologizing to her sister. She'd spent the last two months panicked and sleepless, worried that something bad had happened to her sister. She'd lied to Debra, she created a false persona, all because Nessa didn't bother to leave a note.

"I know," Nessa said. "I know. But I'm back now."

Ramona studied her sister's face. Because they were identical twins born only minutes apart, looking at Nessa had always been like looking in a mirror. They had the same cluster of freckles, the same cute nose, the same dark blue circling their light blue irises. Even their hair was similarly styled and cut.

But she didn't feel that way now. Now, looking at her sister, she saw a completely different person. Nessa didn't look younger than her, per se, but she looked more childlike, less mature. Even the makeup she wore looked like she was trying to compensate for something, like she was a kid trying to pass as an adult. Her smile wasn't very confident. Her gaze wasn't as steady. Perhaps she had changed in the last few months. Or perhaps—

Perhaps Ramona had changed. Perhaps she'd matured in a way that Nessa still hadn't. She'd lived through broken hearts and family drama and loads of issues that Nessa had simply run away from. Ramona was seven minutes older than Nessa, but she suddenly felt years more mature.

"Where were you this whole time?" she asked.

Nessa looked away.

"Please talk to me," Ramona pressed.

"I was … I was staying with friends. On the coast. I know I should've told you, but it was hard for me."

"It was hard for you?" Ramona asked. "I had to stay behind and pick up your pieces. Don't ask me to feel sorry for you."

"I'm not! I—"

"Just tell me why you left."

"Because he picked you!" she shouted. "After the wedding, I realized my mistake. I was ashamed and I couldn't handle it. But … it wasn't fair. He picked you."

"I don't understand."

"You will," she answered. "I should probably go."

Ramona grabbed her sister by the wrist. She'd walked out of her life once before; she wasn't going to do it again. "You're not leaving."

Nessa pulled away. "I'm not. I'm staying here. I just … can't be *here*, you know?" She gestured at McInney Manor looming behind her. "But I promise to call you. Tonight. I'm going to be a part of your life again. I … I promise."

And with that, she walked away. Once again, she left Ramona behind. But this time, she looked over her shoulder as she went. And that made all the difference.

With Nessa once again gone, Ramona became acutely aware that her charade was over. Everybody knew she was the wrong twin. Everybody—even Debra. She looked at all the faces surrounding her, and they were motionless. Everyone stared at the imposter in the dress.

Silence.

Nothing but silence. Inside, Ramona could hear her own pulse. Outside, nothing.

She saw Scott talking to Debra. He was gesturing wildly, trying to explain all these days of lying and pretending. Debra shook her head. Ramona couldn't hear exactly what was being said, and she was thankful for that.

She didn't want to be a part of that argument, but she knew she had to be. Whether she'd intended it or not, she was part of this mess. As she walked through the clusters of party guests, she passed Rob, who diverted his gaze as she walked by.

After what felt like a long walk of shame, Ramona reached Scott and Debra.

"And that's it," he was saying. "We were so worried about you, we just … we lied." He was flailing. He needed Ramona's support.

Silently, she joined them and slipped her hand inside his. "Sorry, Debra."

Debra looked at them, first Scott, then Ramona, then Scott again. In the background, party music continued to play. She waited, seemingly weighing her possible responses, and then she laughed.

"Debra?"

"Mom? Oh God. Is your heart okay?"

Debra doubled over with laughter.

"Mom?"

"Honey, I've known for days. I'm old, not stupid."

"What?" Ramona asked. The party music seemed to fade away, but that was probably just in her head.

Debra stood up and held both their hands so that the three of them formed a circle. "Since you were babies, I always thought you two would grow up and fall in love. I always hoped you would. These last two weeks, I've just been playing along so I could watch you two grow closer together. Now, I love Nessa, don't get me wrong. But come on, everyone knows you two were the real soul mates."

Ramona felt numb. First her sister, then Debra. Everyone seemed to be conspiring to get them together. Either they were destined, or they were so *un*-destined that no amount of matchmaking could bring them together.

"And how's your heart?" Scott asked.

"It's *fine*," Debra said. "It swells whenever I see the two of you."

Scott turned toward Ramona. "I've really made a mess of things, haven't I?"

"We both have," Ramona said.

"So does that mean—?" Debra asked.

Scott squeezed her hand. Ramona was tempted to squeeze back. But she couldn't. "I have to go," she said.

"What?"

"Something always happens," she said. "Every time I'm happy, every time I think this'll be it, something always happens. No matter how many people keep pushing us in the right direction, one of us—you or me, probably you—ends up ruining it. I've lived my life with this sense of hope that everything will turn out okay, but that has never happened. And honestly, I don't think *my* heart can handle that stress anymore.

"So this is your last chance, Scott McInney. I will give you the rest of the day to figure things out. If you have any doubts, don't bother finding me. No judgments either way. You just need to make up your mind. I think we both deserve that."

Ramona walked away from the party, a mixture of fear and excitement building up inside her. She wasn't like Nessa, running away from her problems. She was finally doing things on her own terms.

"Where will you be?" Scott called to her.

She didn't answer. He'd know.

Chapter Seventeen

The party wound down and everybody left. Rob and Jeffrey were on clean-up duties, which included a couple of unpleasant wet spots on the dance floor courtesy of Scott's BLM crew. Hopefully they were just from spilled beers.

Scott volunteered to take Debra to her much awaited hospital check-up, to show support and to distract him from his upcoming life-changing decision.

While Debra checked herself in, Scott walked down the familiar hallway. He'd spent so many sleepless nights here during the last few months. He knew every corner, but something seemed different somehow. Foreign. It was like he'd never stepped inside these walls before.

"Mr. McInney!" someone called from the edge of the hallway.

Scott turned around to see a familiar face: Dr. Nguyen, the young doctor who had been treating Debra since she first came to Farber Memorial. He looked frazzled and busy, as doctors usually do, but he smiled at Scott.

"Dr. Nguyen," Scott said. "We just got here."

"So I heard," the doctor explained. "I was just about to meet with Debra. I trust you've been making sure she hasn't had any issues."

"I tried."

The doctor patted him on the shoulder. "I figured you would."

Scott's eyes shifted to the room at the end of the hall: the waiting room. Had it only been two weeks ago that he'd proposed there in front of total strangers? Debra stood there waiting for them.

"Debra. You look great," Dr. Nguyen said. "I just ran into your son. Come with me and we'll check out your vitals."

• • •

An hour later, X-rays were finished, blood was drawn, and Dr. Nguyen was happy to report that everything looked fine. Scott held his mom's hand and waited for official word that she could go.

"Have you thought about Ramona?" Debra asked.

"Every minute I haven't been worrying about you."

"And?"

"And I shouldn't have put her through all that. She didn't want to lie to you. If I hadn't pushed her—"

"Don't be sorry," she said. "You were trying to help me."

"But it was a stupid idea," he said.

"No argument there," she said. "It was perhaps the dumbest thing you could do in this situation. But, come on. We both know you inherited your father's reasoning skills."

Scott laughed in spite of himself.

"Don't beat yourself up about it, okay?" Debra said. Her voice had all of its strength back. "I understand why you did it. And your heart was in the right place. Just don't ever do anything like that ever again."

He stuck his fingers into the air. "Scout's honor."

She laughed. "You were never a Scout."

The sound of her laughter didn't take away Scott's feelings of regret and guilt. All his careful plans had backfired on him. On everyone. His mother deserved the truth. But he'd made the decision in a moment of weakness, back when Debra's health was definitely in the front of his mind. And once he made that decision, he'd stayed committed to it, for better or worse.

And the end result was definitely in the "for worse" category.

"Oh, don't look so glum," Debra scolded him. "No one's dying."

Scott tried to course-correct his face, turning his frown into a smile, but all he could accomplish was a worried grimace.

"Seriously," Debra said. "Stop fretting about me. You need to figure out what you're going to do about Ramona."

"I already put her through so much. I—"

"Scott Owen McInney," Debra said. That shut him up fast. "I just have one question for you. And you'd better be straight with me."

"I promise."

Debra looked him straight in the eyes, and he saw the strength and confidence that he always expected from his mother. "Scott, who do you love?"

"What do you mean?"

"Tell me the name of the woman you love."

"Ramona," he said. He didn't pause to think. That would've been too dangerous. Besides, his mother knew what he was going to say anyway.

"Honey," she said. "You've done some profoundly stupid things this year. I won't stand by while you add another one to that list."

"You're saying—"

"I'm saying you should go after her. Get the girl, the *right* girl. She gave you some time. You've thought about it. Now go."

He didn't get up. He wanted to. He wanted to jump up and scream Ramona's name from the rooftops and run until he couldn't run anymore. He wanted to give Ramona a big, dramatic ending to their big, dramatic week together. But there was something holding him back.

"You're not running after her," Debra said. Disappointment hung on her wrinkled face.

"Mom, what if I already blew it?"

Even though she was weak, Debra pulled herself forward and placed her hands on Scott's shoulders. "Son," she said. "Listen to me. Please."

"I'm all ears," he said.

"My mother, your Grandma Pat, she had this saying. She used to say it all through my childhood, every time I got my heart broken by the long train of losers that I met before your father. Mom always said to me, 'You can't make someone love you any more than you can make the ocean stand still.' And I believe that. I always have. But I think there's a second half to that saying, too. You can't make someone love you, sure, but you also can't force yourself to love someone you don't. Now, the way I see it, Ramona loves you and you love her just the same. Am I right?"

Scott nodded.

"Then there's your answer," she said, as if it were the simplest thing in the world. "Go get her."

• • •

Scott drove his old Ford all the way across town. As he pulled into her apartment complex, he tried to see if her lights were on, but the curtains were all closed. He ran to her front door and pounded. Again and again.

No answer.

"Ramona!" he shouted.

No answer.

He tried calling her cell again, but it only went to voice message. "Uh, hi. Ramona. I know this is the third message I've left in the last ten minutes, but will you please call me? Soon? I've made up my mind. Finally. We really need to talk. Uh … this is Scott." He clicked off his phone. He knew she wasn't going to pick up.

He also knew, without a shadow of a doubt, that she wasn't in her apartment. And if she wasn't in her apartment, then there was only one other place where she could possibly be: He had to get back to McInney Manor.

The drive to his childhood home took forever. He hit every red light on the way. When he finally pulled up to the house, he could tell that she wasn't inside. The front door was locked, and there was no way she would sneak inside.

So he ran around back, looking for her amongst the remaining party decorations. Some of the balloons still bobbed in the air. Even the speaker system hadn't yet been disassembled and stored away. It was a party with no people. The whole place felt haunted.

And Ramona still wasn't there.

"Ramona!" he called out, hoping for some response. Anything.

He looked all around him—cake, confetti, streamers, and no Ramona. Then he looked up. Their old treehouse loomed overhead. He wasn't sure why he had the sudden realization that she was up there, but he felt her presence. She had to be up there.

Scott didn't believe in intuition, but he certainly felt it right now. He began to climb.

"Ramona!" he shouted.

No answer.

"Ramona!" he shouted again. In his mind, he thought he heard a soft, sweet voice reply, but it was just in his imagination. There was no reply. If she was there—and he certainly felt her there—then she was keeping quiet.

Still, he couldn't give up now, not when he had the fire in his belly, not when he finally understood what his heart really wanted. He climbed the treehouse's rickety steps.

"Ramona!" he called again, once he was halfway up. He'd climbed this tree so often as a child, but now—now, it felt different. It didn't feel smaller, like so many childhood things tended to feel. In fact, it somehow felt bigger, more important. And the treehouse steps seemed to extend upward for miles.

Finally, he reached the trap door and pushed it open. *Please*, he thought. *Let her be here! Let her be here!*

"I thought you'd never come," Ramona said from inside the treehouse. She sat on one of the understuffed bean bag chairs. She had a *Sports Illustrated* in her hands. Its pages were crinkled and its cover boy hadn't pitched for the Diamondbacks in eight years.

"Catching up on some light reading?" he asked.

"Something like that."

God, he was ecstatic to see her. Somehow, he'd known she'd be there, but it didn't make her presence any less exciting. He beamed like an idiot.

She didn't return his smile. Instead, she still looked panicked and hurt.

"Ramona," he said.

"You have your answer."

Scott sighed deeply. "Yes," he said. "I choose you. I've always chosen you."

"But what about Nessa? What about you two and your little treasure chest?"

"I guess that was the big difference between the two of you. She loved that little box for what it looked like, but you were the girl who wanted to open it and look inside."

"What's that supposed to mean?"

He kissed her. The rush of contact was sudden and incredible. The bean bag shifted underneath her, spilling more of its stuffing onto the wooden floor. She grabbed a hold of his shirt.

Scott had certainly felt something the other times he kissed Ramona, but those were all under the disguise of Nessa. This was the first time he kissed Ramona as herself. No secrets, no aliases, no ulterior motives. Just two people kissing, two people holding each other, two people in love.

"I love you, Ramona," he said. He didn't expect those words to come out of his mouth, but he didn't regret them either.

"You sure you're talking to the right sister?" she asked.

He laughed. His thumb rolled lightly along her cheek. He needed to kiss her again, but first he had something to say. "I was an idiot before," he explained. "But I love you. I always have. Sure, Nessa's beautiful, and we have a lot of good memories together, but you're the one I think about at night."

"So why didn't you realize that before?" she asked.

He shook his head. "I don't know. I guess it's because I've always been so comfortable with you. I love hanging out with you so much. I just assumed our friendship was so big, it didn't leave room for anything else. Now I realize that our friendship was just a piece of what we have between us. I don't want Nessa. I don't want you pretending to be anyone else. I want you, Ramona Scapizi. Just you."

He kissed her again, feeling her body melt into his.

"I want you, too," she whispered.

"So that leaves one question," he said.

"And that is?"

"Will you forgive me?"

She squinted at him for the longest moment, and he got the distinct feeling that she was playing with his emotions. Then, to answer his question, she kissed him again.

"So this means you forgive me?" he asked.

"Pretty much."

"You don't know how that makes me feel," he said.

"Oh, I think I have some idea."

Once again, it felt natural when she slipped into his arms, like a missing piece, like a physical part of him. He looked around the treehouse, at those familiar wooden walls and the childhood posters that he'd never had the heart to take down. It seemed so right that they'd finally connected here, of all places. In a way, both their lives had been leading toward this moment.

He smiled a genuine smile for the first time in a long time. And for the first time ever, the woman he loved smiled back.

He could've sat in comfortable silence for the rest of the night, but Ramona asked, "So how will our families react? You know, now that we're together?"

"Well, Mom is stoked," he admitted. "And Nessa's going to be okay. More or less. And I'm going to have a long conversation with Rob and Jeffrey. I'm not sure about them. But I am sure of one thing," he said. His strong arms wrapped around her and pulled her close. The floorboards creaked under the movement, but they were otherwise safe.

"What's that?" she asked.

He laughed, easing his body closer to hers. "I don't think either of us is going to get much sleep tonight."

About the Author

Evan Purcell is an English teacher in rural China. While he misses a few things about America (particularly Starbucks and cheese), he certainly loves the adventure of living in an area with so much history and culture. You can read about his writings and travels at *www.EvanPurcell.Blogspot.com*. And if you ever pass him on the street, please offer him some cheese. He really misses that.

A Sneak Peek from Crimson Romance
(From *Marrying the Wrong Man* by Elley Arden)

"There must be a mistake," Morgan Parrish said, as she blinked at the dull quarter in the palm of her hand.

"No mistake," the perky credit union teller replied. "Up until five seconds ago, the account balance was twenty-five cents."

Morgan's stomach flipped, causing a tidal wave of panic to obliterate rational thought. "That can't be. Check again." She leaned so far over the counter that the teller backed away. "Something is wrong with your screen. You're missing zeros. Lots of zeros. This account was established the day I was born. I've never made a single withdrawal in thirty-two years!"

"But the joint account owner, Kathleen Parrish, has." The young woman, who Morgan had picked expressly because she didn't recognize her, studied her computer screen. "According to our records, she withdrew twenty-five thousand dollars two months ago."

Morgan clawed at the V-neck of her sweater. That was impossible. "My mother hasn't been anywhere near Harmony Falls in years." At least as far as Morgan knew ... but these days she was so far out of the family loop, anything was possible.

Her father's arrest two weeks ago had come as a complete shock. She'd been the last to know he'd been taking bribes for more than five years, even when he'd been mayor of Harmony Falls. And then last week, out of the blue, her mother and uncle disappeared after being traced to an international flight. Why shouldn't she be the last to know her mother fled the country and cleared out the savings account, too?

"Is there a problem?" A familiar voice came from behind the teller.

Morgan cringed. Mary Kemper, the credit union manager, had been one of Morgan's mother's snobby friends. Mary glanced at Morgan only briefly, and for one blissful second, she thanked the lord for that extra thirty pounds she'd been wearing since Charlotte's birth. But then Mary looked up again.

"Morgan Parrish, is that you?" Her eyes widened as she gasped. "Well, I'm … " Her words tapered off as the shock faded, and her natural arrogance reasserted itself with a cold lift of her chin. "Is there a problem?" she asked again, as if—on second thought— she didn't know Morgan Parrish from "Adam." Probably because the daughter of a felon and a potential fugitive wasn't the most respectable person with whom to conduct small talk.

Well, screw that. Morgan only had twelve more hours in this town, and these days, she had more to worry about than what the country club set wagged their tongues about.

"Hi, Mary. How are you?"

"Fine." How could one word be so painful it wrinkled every ounce of real estate on the woman's face?

The teller tapped a perfectly manicured nail against the screen, speaking in a nervous, hushed whisper. "Ms. Parrish was unaware of the large withdrawal made two months ago."

Mary peered at the screen, and her lips curled. "Well, unfortunately, this account does not require signatures of both account holders for withdrawal. Your mother was within her legal boundaries to withdraw the money." She coughed into her hand.

Legal boundaries? Ha! What about moral boundaries? Her mother didn't seem to care about those. And those indiscretions had Morgan in one hell of a bind. "This is bullshit!"

"I'm sure this is a most unpleasant discovery, Ms. Parrish, but there's no need to make a scene." The woman flashed a fake, tight smile at the customer behind Morgan, then stepped closer and lowered her silky voice to a hiss. "Perhaps your mother decided it was the only way to recoup the money she lost on the wedding after you cheated on the groom. Seems to me *that* started the whole downhill spiral for your family—and this town."

Ouch. Not that she didn't deserve that. But when her daddy had been mayor, nobody would've dared to criticize her. What a difference three years made.

Back then, when Daddy said jump, everyone did. Including her. Agreeing to marry the town's favorite son was the biggest leap of all. Too bad she'd never loved Justin Mitchell as much as her daddy did. If she had, she wouldn't have had sex with her ex—the town's bad boy, Charlie Cramer—the night of her bachelorette party and stupidly left that incriminating tiara in his car for his nosy sister, Alice, to find.

"Oh! *Parrish*!" The teller stared at Morgan with a newfound curiosity. "I never made the connection."

Morgan wished she hadn't, but since she had, there was no use shrinking from the fact. "Yep, Parrish. Kind of like the F-word in these parts now, huh?"

Mary sneered. "You have a lot of nerve being flippant, dear. Your father's in jail. Your mother is God knows where. And that plastics plant your family promised would save this town is only half-built and doomed. Do you know how many people had financial ties to the construction alone?"

"My father," the teller interjected. "He was contracted to do electrical work. He had to layoff half his crew when the plant construction stopped."

Some of the other tellers and customers moved closer and all of them were side-eyeing this conversation. Morgan chewed the inside of her cheek. Gossip at the country club was one thing, but she didn't want anyone breaking out pitchforks and torches. Besides, she wasn't proud of the damage her family had caused. It was just that being flippant felt better than being scared and sad.

Morgan held up her hands in a mea culpa. "Look, I'm sorry about your father. Frankly, I'm sorry about mine, too. There were a lot of victims to his schemes." *I should know.* "I don't condone anything he did, and I wasn't a part of it."

The man in line behind her scoffed. "Aren't you legal counsel for your uncle's corrupt corporation?"

She sighed. "No. I never took that job. I'm not even practicing law anymore." She'd been fired for taking too much time off when Charlotte had gotten sick with all those recurring ear infections. Which was why she'd needed this money. Without it, she wasn't sure what came next.

Knowing when the fight was lost, Morgan turned and simply walked out of the bank.

It wasn't until she was settling back behind the wheel of the Jaguar her daddy'd bought her as a law school graduation present, staring at the beyond-empty gas gauge, that she let her fate sink in.

She was doomed—payback for lying to Justin, cheating with Charlie, and the general self-absorbed bitchiness she'd spread around town before she left.

Karma sucked.

Please, tell me we're even now. "Please," she whispered as she glanced at the sky. How was she ever going to move on with her life if she kept getting dragged back down?

Her answer was a big fat splat on her windshield, courtesy of a low-flying pigeon.

Straightening her wilted posture on a deep breath, Morgan glanced in the rearview mirror at the empty car seat. She needed to get back to Charlotte. Aunt Phyllis was a stranger to the toddler, and that house—Morgan cringed—was barely fit for the cats let alone a two-year-old.

She probably should have taken Charlotte with her—a lady with a baby got more sympathy, at least—but she couldn't risk anyone seeing Charlotte until Charlie knew about the little girl.

Morgan dropped her head to the steering wheel and moaned. This was not how things were supposed to go. She was *supposed* to lay low at Aunt Phyllis's for a couple days, withdraw the money from the savings account, beg for Charlie's forgiveness, so her conscience would quiet, and decide where to go next. What was she supposed to do now? Extend her stay at Aunt Phyllis's?

Living in Hell would be happier for a Parrish than living in Harmony Falls.

The angry red service engine light popped on again, taunting her.

Considering Morgan hadn't kept up with regular maintenance on the car, she'd be lucky if she could make it out of town, even if she had someplace else to go. Whatever was causing the engine light to glow would certainly eat up most—if not all—of the measly thousand dollars that remained from selling off almost everything she'd owned.

She slammed the heel of her hand against the steering wheel, giving it a violent shake. *Stupid car.* She couldn't even afford to take care of it anymore. She should've sold it to the senior partner at the law firm when he'd offered to buy it.

Morgan's eyes widened. Wait a minute. Maybe she could still sell it. If Bryce Becker over at Becker's Car and Truck would buy the Jag for, say, $25,000, then Morgan could buy a newer, cheaper car and pocket the rest. Hell, if she could walk away with $10,000 after unloading this car and buying a new one, she'd still have enough to sign a lease on a small apartment somewhere far away from this town and her family's unfolding legal drama.

Hope was not lost, yet.

But it sure did start to slip ten minutes later when Bryce glared at her from across the used car lot. "Well, looky here. A fox has returned to the hen house." He hiked the shiny black belt holding up baggy dress pants over his beer belly. "I'm surprised a Parrish has the guts to show up in this town again."

Here we go. "It's nice to see you, too." They'd been friends once. Even went to a homecoming dance freshman year.

"I wish I could say the same, I do. But your daddy screwed us over good. Promising to get that plastics plant and all them jobs for us. Said he'd do more as a congressman than Justin Mitchell ever did, and he'd take Harmony Falls along for the ride." Bryce snickered. "Well, he took us for a ride, alright. All the way to prison."

She gritted her teeth. "I don't agree with what my father did." She didn't even know the details. Their relationship had become irreparable the minute she refused to beg Justin to go through with the wedding. "In fact, I haven't spoken to him since I left Harmony Falls."

"And yet, here you are, still behind the wheel of Daddy's fancy car."

"Actually, I want to sell it." *I have to sell it.* But it was never good to show desperation on a used car lot.

Bryce's bushy eyebrows rose. "Is that so?"

He stalked the vehicle. When he peered into the backseat, Charlotte's car seat seemed to glow like a homing beacon. *Crap.* She should've talked to Charlie before she went to the bank. The last thing she needed was some townie running off to tell him Morgan was here … with a child when he'd spent the last two years thinking she'd placed their baby for adoption.

She bit into her bottom lip as Bryce's eyebrows rose.

"You got yourself a little one, huh?"

Morgan nodded but refused to take the bait.

"You know, Justin's the mayor now, happily married to Alice Cramer." He kept his beady little eyes on the car, opening the driver's side door and plopping onto the seat. "And uh, your other *old pal* Charlie Cramer runs a fancy restaurant in town." He cut his gaze to her, and it was equal parts suspicion and expectation. "You stay in touch with any of them?"

He was fishing for information about the car seat, wasn't he?

The sweat dripping down her back had nothing to do with the warmer-than-usual May temperature. Three years ago, she'd stood on Charlie's front porch and announced her pregnancy just days after Justin had left her at the altar. Alice, Charlie's sister, had always held a torch for Justin and animosity that Morgan seemingly stood in their way. Man, what a convoluted mess their lives must've been for anyone on the outside looking in—and there were a lot of curious people in Harmony Falls. The minute those people got wind of Charlotte, the speculation would begin. *Is she Justin's? Is she Charlie's?*

Morgan couldn't blame them for that. She'd been a spoiled, unhappy young woman, wanting it all and used to getting what she wanted. And she'd wanted Charlie Cramer, even if she already had Justin Mitchell. Her fiancé's congressional schedule put him in Washington for weeks at a time paving the way back to Charlie's backseat for a handful of desperate transgressions exactly nine months prior to Charlotte's arrival

"I haven't stayed in touch with anyone," she said. "I've been busy." First, hiding the pregnancy from her father and mother, who would've pressured her into an abortion had they known she was pregnant with the wrong man's baby. Then, raising her little girl with no family support, because her parents deemed their wayward daughter and illegitimate grandchild a liability to dear old dad's political career.

He gave her a shitty grin. "Maybe you'll get to bump into them while you're here."

God, she hoped not. She didn't want to bump into Justin and Alice—ever. And she wanted her visit with Charlie to go as smoothly as possible, a carefully planned operation.

"Can we skip the small talk and get down to business?" she asked.

"I can give you ten grand for the car," he said.

Ten thousand dollars was a far cry from the twenty-five thousand she'd been hoping for. "Is that because the car is really worth that much, or because I'm a Parrish and you want to stick it to me?"

"The engine light is on. The mileage is sky high. The tires are bald. And that's just what I can see. If this vehicle belonged to my mama, she'd be offered ten grand, too." He pushed off the steering wheel and stood beside the car. "Unlike some of us, I'm not in the business of screwing people over."

The jab actually made Morgan feel a bit better. At least she wasn't being cheated. "Okay. I'll take the ten grand, but now I need another car. What's the cheapest reliable vehicle on the lot?"

Bryce put his hands on his hips and puffed out his chest while he scanned the cars. "I can do $9,000 out the door on that red one over there, but not a penny less."

The snub-nosed, boxy-looking economy car paled in comparison to the long, sleek, sexy curves of her Jaguar. She didn't want to drive something that looked like a clown car. She especially didn't want to hand over almost all of the money she'd just made. "Nine thousand dollars for that leaves me with a measly grand." Plus the grand she already had. She might be able to afford first and last months' rent on $2,000, but it wouldn't leave much room for error. "How about $8,000?"

"Now, don't go getting snobby on me. She might not be the prettiest car on the lot, but with factory warranty and low mileage, that there's a gem. I can't just give it away."

He was enjoying this, wasn't he?

When he waved at someone behind them, Morgan cringed, sinking her head into her shoulders. *Please, don't be someone who knows me.* She'd had about all the vitriol she could take for one day.

"Deal or no deal?" he asked.

"Deal." She'd get over the vehicle's ugliness as long as it wouldn't shake apart into a million pieces on the highway or anything. "Let's go to your office so we can get this done."

Once she'd signed on the dotted line, some way, somehow, Morgan Parrish was getting the hell out of Harmony Falls—again.

• • •

Charlie Cramer's pick-up truck guzzled oil the way he used to guzzle Jack.

Or beer. Or any other alcohol that found its way into his hands.

He shook his head as he detoured from Main Street and pulled into Becker Car and Truck, thankful for more than a thousand days of sobriety. He had his dream job as chef at Char-Grilled Bistro. His sister was happily married. Life as a once pitiful, laughable Cramer had taken a damn good turn. *Finally.*

But maybe he'd spoken too soon.

A white Jaguar with Connecticut plates parked on Bryce's lot. Charlie hit the brakes and rubbed his eyes until they burned. Apparently, there was a downside to sobriety—too many dry days caused hallucinations.

It had to be a hallucination, because that looked like Morgan Parrish's car. He had spent the better part of a year in pursuit of that car and its driver.

With hands clenched around the wheel, he drove straight at the figment of his imagination. At the last minute, he chickened out and turned the wheel. What if it was real? What if Morgan Parrish came back to town?

Son of a bitch. When she'd left town with his baby in her belly, after Justin dropped her cold, Charlie had followed. He'd hoped she would give them a chance to be happy together like they'd been that summer between her freshman and sophomore years in college, before her father stepped in and broke them apart.

But once he'd reached her in Connecticut, she'd refused to talk to him except to threaten a restraining order. So he backed down, got sober, and enrolled in culinary school. Then, the baby had been born and he'd received papers to declare paternity. Charlie scratched an itch over his heart. He didn't fight Morgan's wish to place the child for adoption. As a newly recovered alcoholic, he'd been the last person on earth who should've been a father. And Morgan was no prize, either.

He touched the gritty surface of the white car—just to make sure it was real—and then he headed straight for Bryce's office. If she did have the nerve to show her face in this town again, he had a few things to say.

As he weaved through racks of auto parts and man-sized stacks of tires, the soles of Charlie's cowboy boots echoed. He needed oil and then he needed to get to the bistro for dinner prep. He *didn't* need this aggravation. Pushing the Mitchell family to invest in a small restaurant instead of the bakery they'd proposed meant there was a lot riding on his success.

And it'd been slow to come.

"Afternoon, Charlie," Roberta Urlacher called from behind the checkout counter. "What's on the menu this week? More of that veal? Rudy can't stop talking about it."

"No veal. This week I have duck."

She crinkled her nose. "Ew. Duck is slimy and tough."

"Only when it's cooked by someone who shouldn't be cooking it," he said. "Is Bryce in?"

"Bryce is, uh, closing a deal. Can I help you with something?"

"Oil," he said without taking his eyes off Bryce's office door.

"You use a 5w20 in her, right?"

"Yes." He leaned against the counter, wishing it was a bar.

"Be back in a jiff."

A few seconds later, Charlie heard a door click open and the words, "Good luck to you."

He met Bryce's wide eyes as the man exited his office with a woman behind him. Charlie's heart hammered against his rib cage. She wore her dark hair in a ponytail—something Morgan never did—and the baggy sweatshirt was wrong, too. But he'd have known that face anywhere.

Her mouth opened when she saw him. Maybe his did, too. He was so numb he couldn't feel a damn thing except the vicious thrashing in his chest.

"Well, well, Charlie Cramer, isn't this a surprise?" Bryce grinned. "I'll be right with you."

Morgan stepped toward Charlie, looking different enough he couldn't help but stare. It took him a few seconds to realize she wasn't wearing makeup—not a stitch. For a woman who used to leave smudges of color on his white T-shirts after a hug, it was a shocking change. Was she sick? He used to pray she'd pay for agreeing to that wedding her father wanted and choosing Justin over him, then leaving town the minute they actually got their chance to be together. But he didn't want her to be ill.

"Charlie," she rasped. "I'm … " her mouth closed, and he watched the muscles of her throat move as she swallowed, "visiting my aunt."

Which was weird, too. The high and mighty Parrishes had stayed far away from Kitty's reclusive sister, Phyllis.

"5w20," Roberta said. Her voice ended in a whoop, and the plastic container thudded loudly on the counter.

He might have things to say to Morgan, but he wasn't going to say them here in front of an eager audience.

Reaching into his back pocket, he grabbed his wallet and tossed a twenty onto the counter. "Thanks, Roberta."

"I'm going to call you," Morgan said.

Charlie clenched his jaw. *Two years too late.* He gave Morgan a curt nod but otherwise stood stock still until she and Bryce left the building.

"I should've warned you." Roberta handed him his change. "I was hoping they'd stay in the office long enough for you to get out without seeing her. It must be hard. Is that the first time you've seen her since she left town? "

Charlie's nostrils flared. He didn't like to share details about his life or talk about his feelings with people close to him. He sure as hell wasn't going down that road with an auto parts store cashier. *Small towns.* These people needed to mind their own business.

A growl caught in the back of his throat as he retreated.

It wasn't until he stepped out of the building, clutching the quart of oil, that his head cleared enough to go on the attack again. *Phone call, my ass.* He wasn't waiting around to hear from her.

Charlie jumped into his truck and headed for Phyllis Marion's farmhouse. They had unfinished business.